THERE'S A BADGE FOR THAT

RELLY MORING

ISBN-13: 978-1-9992425-0-3 (Paperback)

ISBN-13: 978-1-9992425-1-0 (Ebook)

Any references to historical events, real people, or real places are used fictitiously. Names, characters, and places are products of the author's imagination.

Epigraph excerpt from WHEN THE WORLD TIPS OVER by Jandy Nelson, copyright © 2024 by Jandy Nelson. Used by permission of Dial Books for Young Readers, an imprint of Penguin Young Readers Group, a division of Penguin Random House LLC & reproduced by permission of Walker Books Ltd, London, SE11 5HJ www.walker.co.uk. All rights reserved.

Book design by Christian Storm.

First printing edition 2025.

Sol Books

www.SolBooks.ca

BEFORE YOU READ

CONTENT WARNINGS

There's a Badge for That contains mature themes intended for older audiences. Specific references include domestic violence, suicide, and sexual assault. Readers should use discretion.

LANGUAGE CONSIDERATIONS

There's a Badge for That begins in the early '90s and some of the language used accurately reflects the acceptable vocabulary of the time. Terms chosen to encapsulate the decade authentically, such as "psych ward" and "crazy" are not intended to demean, or evoke negative feelings.

This book also honours Canadian English, so any perceived "misspellings" you spot are intentional, not typos.

GETTING HELP

You are not alone. Please see the RESOURCES section at the end of this book for support.

For my real life camp friends. I hope you love the pieces of yourselves that you find between these pages.

And for my children. May you breathe that same wild air and find your truest selves in the freedom of little cabins amongst the trees.

Find the people who plant the sun in your chest.

JANDY NELSON

PART ONE
JUMPER

CHAPTER 1
AUGUST 1994
MELODY

Two hours to go. Melody's body vibrated with anticipation throughout the lengthy drive to Camp Sweet Clover. She had been away far too long after skipping her final year as a camper because her friends had teased her about summer camp being juvenile. Now, after enduring a nightmarish ninth grade year, she couldn't care less what they thought. She was desperate to get back to her second home; the place she had first fallen in love with three years earlier, and the only place she truly felt like herself.

She had made friends there that she'd never have been able to make back home, especially after her parents had moved her family one town over and everyone there acted "too cool" for... well, everything. Her new school friends were already drinking, smoking, and hooking up with boys, and Melody didn't even have any boobs. Her doctor said to blame it on the years she starved herself skinny as a gymnast. *Lame.* Kalliope and her other childhood friends were still a big part of her life, but it was a lot of work to try to coerce a ride out of her parents every weekend.

Sweet Clover had always been her escape. She forgot about friend drama, boy drama, parent drama, her self-esteem issues—

everything just melted away when she got close to her summer home and smelled the intoxicating camp air. Melody, fifteen now, had returned to CSC to volunteer for a week. She could visit without having to take care of an entire cabin full of kids, and she was even knocking out the volunteer hours she needed for school. A win-win in her mind. A perfect summer getaway laid before her.

Her parents cranked the AC to combat the balmy August day, but Melody opened her window to let in the smell of pine trees, mossy earth, and the lake off in the distance. The breeze blew her dirty blonde hair behind her, while she squinted her eyes shut to protect them from the sun barrelling in through the treetops. Even decades into the future, Melody would get whiffs of camp when the season, surroundings, and weather were just right, and it would transport her back to this time and place.

The dirt road leading into camp proved unkind to their old minivan, and Melody wondered if her parents would make it back out again. Unlike previous years, Melody's nerves eased the instant she pulled into the parking lot. Bounding out of the car, she fell into the arms of two previous counsellors at once.

"Melody! Your hair is so long!" Megan exclaimed.

"You look so grown up, girl!" Suzy said.

Melody tried not to roll her eyes. As something akin to staff now, she hoped they would treat her appropriately, not like an annoying little sister their mother forced them to take along. Once she ran into a few younger friends from previous years, Daniel and Albert, Melody realized where Megan and Suzy were coming from. The boys looked so grown up to her! They squeezed her tighter than anyone had in a long time, and she didn't want to let go, even if it was getting awkward.

"Hi, guys!" Melody said. "It's so great to see you. It's been forever! I want to catch up, one sec!"

Melody ran back to her parents and hugged them goodbye.

She no longer let them walk her into camp. That was one thing even she was too cool for.

"Have fun, be safe!" her mum shouted as Melody skipped across the parking lot.

"Love you. See you in later!" her dad called.

Melody waved a hand over her head without looking back, and the camp culture swallowed her whole. The boys recapped their last year while she listened, and Albert dragged her giant duffle bag down the hill, covering it with dirt and stains that would later require some serious elbow grease to remove. There were campers and counsellors mulling about everywhere. Some she recognized, and some she didn't.

Melody let Albert and Daniel go on ahead, grateful she didn't have to haul her own bag, and wandered into the centre of the camp to take in the moment on her own. The trees towered over her, swaying gently. A woodpecker tapped his beak through the bark of one, looking for lunch, and when Melody closed her eyes, she heard the faint sound of the lake meeting the shore with the gentle laps of the waves. There it was; the calm that she hadn't felt in months, maybe since the last time she was at CSC.

Eventually, Melody opened her eyes and, while looking around for where to go, spotted a guy a few years older than her sitting on the Fraser Bunkie porch at the bottom of the hill. He had golden blonde hair and a bright smile that seemed familiar, despite not remembering his name.

"Hey, Melody?" He waved at her.

Melody nodded as she approached him.

"Hi, I'm Jack!"

Jack, of course. He'd been a boys' counsellor for a few years, but she couldn't recall an actual conversation with him. Almost as if her body sensed this was a life-altering moment, a flurry of racing thoughts slipped right in under her skin and fear washed over her. *No, not today.* She had left all these brain-games at home.

"Hey!" she said, in the bravest voice she could muster.

Jack beamed at her. "I'm in charge of the volunteers this summer, and this week, that is you!"

Melody just nodded, struggling to multi-task while attempting to overcome her brain's internal meltdown.

"We'll be working on projects together—whatever needs doing around camp. I hope that's okay! I promise, I'll try to make it fun. You're going to be sleeping upstairs in the bunkie. There's another volunteer that arrived last week named Piper. She's in the room next to yours, and then Tanner's been here all summer with me. Do you know Tanner? We have the main floor bedrooms."

Melody tried to keep her eyes from bulging out of her head at the mention of Piper's name, remembering how they crossed paths years ago, and Melody had been so drawn to her, even though they'd never had the chance to get to know each other.

It must be the same Piper, it's not like it's a very common name. She nodded and smiled as Jack talked. He seemed friendly enough, and she figured working with him wouldn't be so bad, but she hoped there would be lots of downtime too to just enjoy camp life.

Jack left Melody to unpack and settle in before lunch. He loved to chat, it seemed, but she wasn't able to reciprocate much at the time. She'd get another chance later. Melody pulled out her brand new Discman, a fifteenth birthday gift, and put on her headphones. Unpacking always needed music. In fact, practically every minute of her life needed music. Despite the punk rock blasting in her ears, Melody still heard someone stomping up the creaky loft stairs.

She froze in place as she heard the other door open and slam, before someone flopped down on the bed. Because the top of the shared dividing wall didn't connect to the vaulted, cobwebbed ceiling, these bedrooms lacked sound-dampening. But who cared about that? The important thing was that Piper was right next door.

Melody waited an appropriate amount of time before she crept out of her room and knocked.

"Hello?" the girl on the other side said.

"Hey, I just unpacked beside you. I wanted to introduce myself," Melody explained through the closed door.

She heard shuffling, then the door swung open. Piper leaned on the knob as if Melody had a split second to make a point before she slammed it again. They looked at each other, and Melody slid into a flashback from the first time their eyes met. Piper had been at CSC during Melody's first year—1991. A year older, Piper had been a tiny preteen girl drowning in too-big clothing. Melody even recalled the exact tie dye shirt she wore. Piper's muddy brown hair had hung around her face in tangles, almost completely obscuring her big green eyes glistening with tears, as a furious man dragged her up the hill to the parking lot. The girls' gaze locked for only a moment as they passed each other, but Melody sensed there was something between them. She knew it wouldn't be the last time she would see Piper.

The girl, likely exasperated by Melody's silence, said, "I'm Piper."

Melody snapped back to reality.

"Hey, I'm Melody."

She looked nothing like the Piper of years past. Her clothes fit her well, though they weren't current styles other girls their age wore, more like hand-me-downs from an older cousin. Piper had pulled her brown hair back into a neat ponytail and looked much older now, but Melody would recognize those green eyes anywhere.

"Are you okay? Your stomping sounded pretty angry."

Looking Melody up and down, Piper replied, "You wouldn't get it."

"I might get more than you'd expect."

"You and your perfect life? I don't think so," Piper spat.

Melody gaped at her. She had never even had a conversation

with Piper, but already the girl was making assumptions about her. *Sure, I may not have it as tough as Piper, but that doesn't mean my life is perfect.*

After a moment of stunned silence, Melody held her tongue and let it be. She didn't want to come on too strong with Piper, a virtual stranger, but inexplicably, she was desperate to get acquainted. Perhaps because she had planned to work as a journalist one day, or maybe she was just plain nosey, but she was dying to find out more about Piper's life. Melody had never met anyone outside her little white picket-fence small town, and she had an insatiable curiosity about what life would be like in other places. *Wait. I was supposed to be leaving the drama back in suburbia where it belonged.*

"Well, I'll let you get back to whatever you were doing. I just wanted to say hi. I'll see you later!" Melody said.

She forced a smile, gave a quick wave, and retreated to her own room.

Piper grunted something that sounded like, "Later," and shut the door.

AUGUST 1994
MELODY

Melody found Piper outside the bunkie later that afternoon. The spot drew many of the volunteers and staff—who weren't currently in charge of children—to hang out during their free time. Besides the dining hall, it was the biggest porch at camp, and the wood railings made for perfect seats, despite a few wobbly spots. Piper sat on the stairs, biting her nails. She must have caught Melody looking, because she spun her body to obscure Melody's view of her face. It was quite obvious, however, at least to Melody, that she was crying.

Melody crept over to the stairs like she was trying not to spook a wild animal, and whispered, "Piper? What's wrong?"

Piper rolled her eyes while she furiously wiped the tears from her cheeks with the back of her hand, as if annoyed Melody was prying again. "I just got a phone call from my grandma. My little brother is in a coma."

"Oh my gosh! I'm so sorry. What happened?" Melody sat down next to Piper.

Piper's sad eyes morphed into those of a dragon as she shouted, "I don't want to talk about it!" before running off down the path towards the waterfront.

Melody wasn't sure what to do. She was worried about Piper, but she also understood what it was like to want to be alone and to not have people respect that. Melody decided it was best to leave her with her feelings, so she moved to find Jack and begin their first project instead.

It didn't take her long to catch him exiting the office door on the dining hall porch. Unlike the bunkie porch, no one congregated there unless it was time to eat. With the proximity to the office, there was always an adult in earshot, so it wasn't exactly an enticing spot. Jack had a boombox in one hand, and paintbrushes in the other. She hoped they'd be doing something fun, like lying in the sun by the lake, but Jack clearly had other plans.

"Oh, hey!" he said when he noticed her. "We're painting the boys' bathroom!"

Melody tried her best not to groan, though the way he smirked at her implied her face was saying it all, so she let her dissatisfaction escape, anyway. Jack laughed so loud with a chortle that warmed her bones, and she said a silent goodbye to the heaviness of her interaction with Piper as it slipped away.

"Come on," Jack called as he walked up the wooded path to the bathroom. "It'll be fun!"

And though she never would have guessed it, he was right.

They spent the afternoon blasting music from the boombox, echoing its way around the cement block bathroom. A space typically full of stinky, pre-pubescent boys, now just the two of them. The paint fumes even covered up the pee smell, mostly. *How is it that boys can't hit a urinal? Come on.* They did their best to keep the paint on the walls and the songs in their mouths, but the paint ended up in their hair and on their shirts, and their mouths filled with laughter instead.

Melody knew in her heart that "camp people" were her people, however, the quick connection with Jack was a pleasant surprise. He was eighteen to Melody's fifteen, and although it wasn't a large age gap, they were in very different stages of life. That didn't seem to matter to the pair, however, and they kept the conversation flowing naturally between them. They chatted about high school. Melody was about to head into grade ten, and Jack, having just graduated, heading off to college in the fall.

"What are you studying at school?" Melody asked Jack.

"I have no clue what I want to do with my life. How is anyone supposed to make that decision at this age?"

Melody nodded. "How about an easier one, then? What's your favourite food?"

"Tacos, but now that I've had them in Mexico, they're not the same here!"

"Oh, I can imagine!" Melody said with a laugh.

"What's your favourite colour?" Jack questioned.

"That's so hard. There are so many good ones. Can I say rainbow?"

Jack smiled. "Do you prefer movies or books?"

Horrified, Melody gaped at him. "As if there's any comparison?"

"I was testing you. You're right. Books over everything."

"But what about music? Where does that fall in?" Melody wondered aloud.

This question stumped Jack, and he was still searching for his answer when Melody heard a commotion outside the bathroom. It sounded like people were standing on the various pathways that split around the building. They were speaking in loud, frantic voices.

"Where might she have gone?"

"Why would she run off?"

"Who else might know where she is?"

"Anyone have any idea who she may have talked to?"

"Has anyone checked the cabin?"

"She's not in a cabin, dude!"

The various voices were indistinguishable, but Melody was

certain they were talking about Piper. She wondered if she should go out and see what the commotion was, but the bathroom was almost finished, and Jack hadn't seemed to pay much attention to the conversation happening outside the building. *I'll quickly finish here before I investigate.*

Jack kept trying to engage her in conversation, but Melody was too distracted. She didn't want Jack to think she was a flake for abandoning him, but she couldn't focus on anything besides the situation just outside their walls. Melody always struggled to make quick decisions, or, like this time, second guessed herself once she'd decided.

"Are you okay?" he prompted.

"Um, I'm not sure. I heard those people outside saying they're looking for someone, and I think they might have meant Piper. I saw her run off earlier."

"You did?"

"Yeah, a phone call from home upset her. They said her brother was in a coma."

"Oh," Jack started, "she has a rough home life. If you saw which way she ran off, maybe you should go help look. I can finish this up. I'll see you at dinner."

"Okay. Thanks, Jack," Melody said as she climbed down the ladder and offered him a quick smile.

When she reached the bunkie, she found a small group of people mulling around, wringing their hands, speaking in hushed voices. Melody joined the group without hesitation and asked what happened.

"We have to find Piper," Daniel said.

"I'm afraid she's going to hurt herself," whispered Cody, a counsellor in training. She remembered him from her years as a camper, though, like Jack, she had spent no time with him. Boys and girls were so segregated at camp, it always seemed outdated to her.

A guy slightly older than Melody rushed out of the building breathless, "she's in her room!"

The group breathed a collective sigh of relief, though the messenger's creased brow didn't relax.

"Uh, I assumed someone had checked there already..." Melody trailed off, wondering how they missed that crucial step.

"What is it, Tanner?" Cody asked.

Ah, that's Tanner.

"She won't open the door. She just yelled at me to go away. I'm worried about what she's doing in there, given her history."

"What do you mean, her history?" Albert asked.

Tanner flashed Cody a worried look, and Melody easily inferred what they were talking about. They must know Piper pretty well.

Remembering that the walls were independent of the vaulted ceiling, Melody figured it wouldn't be hard to climb up on the railing and hoist herself into the rafters.

"I've got this," she called as she ran into the building and up the steep wooden staircase to their bunkie loft.

When she reached the top, she threw her leg onto the stair railing, pulled up and brought herself into a squatted position on top of it. Melody stood gingerly and grabbed the first rafter within her reach, and hoisted herself onto it on her belly, her heart now pounding both from physical exertion and her distress over what she might find in the bedroom.

Melody dragged her body along beam by beam until she had a sightline into the room. Thundering footsteps of teen boys arrived at the top of the stairs, asking what was happening and if Piper seemed okay, but Melody couldn't say a word. The shock paralyzed her.

Piper was in fact in her room. Melody saw her lying on the bed, unmoving.

"Something's wrong," she tried to say, but no noise came out.

Melody's body refused to move, frozen still as a statue, so she moved her eyes to scan the room instead. She noticed a small red stain under Piper's wrist, and it spread every second that passed.

Finally, Melody's adrenaline kicked in. Her confused brain snapped to attention, and she realized she had to move, immediately. Pulling herself into a sitting position on the beam, she hung her legs down between them, and drawing on her childhood experience as a gymnast, easily slipped down into the room, hanging from the beam until her feet almost reached the floor. Melody dropped with a thud while the four guys continued shouting behind her.

She grabbed a t-shirt from the floor and wrapped it around Piper's wrist as tightly as possible, before flinging the door open and instructing Cody to grip the wrist while she made sure Piper was still breathing. The medical drama she watched on TV was paying off. She just hoped it would be enough. *I have this, right?*

"Get Nurse Raina in here now!" Melody shrieked at no one in particular. Tanner turned and ran in response.

Because they were so far outside town, it would take too long for an ambulance to reach them. Therefore, out of an abundance of caution, the camp stocked the nurse's quarters for any conceivable emergency, and their medical staff had extensive training. Nurse Raina would have the medicine to coagulate Piper's blood, and the supplies to stitch up and bandage her wrist. Cuts like this always looked worse than they were, Melody reminded herself. Piper would be fine. *We will save her.*

CHAPTER 3
AUGUST 1994

MELODY

It was already evening when Melody left the room. She had wanted to be there for Piper. No longer out of nosiness, but to be a friend. Thanks to her quick work and Nurse Raina's efforts, Piper didn't need an emergent trip to the hospital, though Melody wondered if she'd end up there, regardless. Either way, Piper was stable and conscious, and her grandma would soon pick her up.

Nurse Raina sent Melody to eat with the dinner bell, but her unease was incessant and her appetite non-existent. Instead, she laid in her bed next door to the almost-crime scene. She kept picturing all the blood and Piper's pale skin, and wondering what would have happened if she had left the bathroom even five minutes later. Melody kept hoping someone, Jack or Tanner, would come check on her, because she was definitely not okay.

This. This is life for the "other" kids. Melody had gotten the taste she had craved to placate her curiosity, and now she would do anything to take it all back.

Eventually drifting off, Melody woke to a noise outside her door. Her heart raced, but as she listened to the voices, she realized it was Piper's grandma and Nurse Raina talking.

"Her daddy beat the boy black and blue. It's a miracle he's even alive. They can't say if he'll make it out of the coma, though. I called Piper to tell her today. That must have set her off. Perhaps I shouldn't have called." Piper's grandma's voice shook, like she was on the verge of tears.

Piper had been dozing in her bed, her body trying to recover from the day's events when Melody left. She listened to shuffling, which must have been the women working to pack up Piper's things to take her home.

"I have to get her proper help. She can't come home with me like this," her grandma continued.

The implication was clear—Piper would go to a hospital instead of home. *She will be heartbroken when she realizes.*

Melody found no escape from her unsettled stomach and racing heart, but did drift back to sleep. The unease followed her into her dreams and she woke up screaming in the night. Still, no one came to check on her. *Where are Tanner and Jack? Can't they hear me from down the stairs?* Melody's loneliness consumed her.

The last time she woke, she heard sobs downstairs in one of the bedrooms. Melody debated for a long time whether she should go downstairs or ignore it and try to go back to sleep. As the crying got louder and included hushed whispers, her heart decided, knowing she'd never get back to sleep not knowing.

Melody pulled on her track pants and slid her feet into her shower flip-flops before she crept down the stairs. She paused at the bottom just long enough to decipher which room the noise had come from, because lights were trailing out under both the doors. *Tanner's room.*

Shuffling over to the door so as not to make the flip flap noise of her sandals on the wood floor, Melody knocked and waited until she heard someone walking towards the door. Tanner opened it a crack and whispered, "Sorry to wake you. Cody's having a rough time."

"Can I join you?"

Cody must have nodded because the door opened for her. Cody sat curled up in a ball on the floor with his arms wrapped around his knees, wearing only basketball shorts and dirty sneakers. She hesitated for a moment before she sat down beside him and wrapped her arms around him. He tried to give her a grateful smile, but the tears kept coming, and his brown eyes looked painfully beet red. His shaggy, almost-black hair laid plastered to his cheeks from his tears.

"Cody, it's okay. She's okay," Melody whispered.

Cody shook his head but didn't say a word. He must have known in his heart that Piper wasn't okay. Melody may have saved her this time, but there was a high probability of this happening again, especially if it had happened before. Melody didn't have all the information.

"Do you really believe she'll be safe at home? Her home was already not a good place, and I don't want her going back there. They won't take care of her; they can't even take care of themselves. Most of the time they did more harm than good, and they are part of the reason this happened in the first place!" Cody whisper-shouted at them.

"But Cody," Melody started, "it's unlikely that she went home."

He let out a wail like something Melody had never heard. *He hadn't already realized that?* She found it hard to understand why Cody wouldn't have been fighting to get up those stairs every minute after the incident if he cared that much for Piper.

Tanner held Cody in a tight hug as he tried to piece together words between panicked gasps.

"They would take her to the hospital. With everything going on with her brother and dad, her grandma has too much on her plate to care for a suicidal teenager too," Melody said.

Cody cried harder.

"How will I talk to her if she's in the hospital? I'm pretty sure they don't allow phone calls in the psych ward! She can't get committed. She won't survive it."

"Uh, that's the only way she might survive this, Cody," Tanner said with hesitation. "The hospital is the safest place for her."

It seemed like every minute they comforted Cody, they took one step forward and two steps back. His sobs kept coming between the irrational sentences he spit out like they burned his tongue. Melody didn't know him well enough to come up with the right words to say, but she wanted to stay and help. She looked at Tanner for guidance.

"Sometimes people need to experience something like this before they realize they do, in fact, want to live. Before they can start over. Before things can get good. Sometimes it takes a lot of hard things, a lot of trauma, before you can see the light at the end of the tunnel. Sometimes, it takes deciding you cannot go on living and trying to end it all, to realize how much you have to live for," Tanner explained.

Cody and Melody stared at him. It seemed like he had a little more experience with this topic than one might expect from just looking at him. Melody realized she had a lot to learn about the realities of other kids her age.

"I've never shared why I go by Tanner instead of Richard," he continued. "All the guys at school got it into their heads that I'm not straight, so instead of calling me Richard, they used the short form, Dick, but meanly, always pairing it with a comment about other guys."

Again, Cody and Melody just looked on with confusion. Melody broke the silence with her meek, nervous voice, "Are you? Not straight, I mean?"

Tanner snickered and his eyes lit up. "Wasn't it obvious?"

A grin crept across Cody's face and Melody laughed too. "Well, now that you mention it," she joked.

It was a welcome distraction, and a relief to see Cody had stopped crying.

"I'm sorry you get bullied at school," Melody said to Tanner as she rested a tentative hand on his arm in condolence.

"It's okay. It was at the end of elementary school. Once I got to high school, things got a lot easier. There were a lot more kids like me there. I didn't feel so alone. Plus, the bullies had a whole new pool of kids to choose from, so I got left alone."

Melody recalled her first year of high school, and it made sense how that would be the case. So many great kids had to deal with such hard things, and it hurt her heart. It didn't seem fair.

"What happened? Before you got to high school, I mean," she asked.

"I struggled with my identity and, of course, the bullying I experienced because of it. I stopped eating, stopped sleeping, and after a while my physical and mental health were so bad that I stopped even going to school. Thankfully, I never tried to take a shortcut to the underworld, though for a while I took a lot of medications to numb the pain, and I very well might have overdosed if I wasn't careful. My mom noticed what was going on, and she sent me to a psychiatrist who recommended an inpatient program at the hospital for a while."

Melody was silent in disbelief. This bubbly, fun, outgoing person had endured so much pain, and may very well have not been here today. She had trouble wrapping her head around that. Grateful that wasn't the case, she did what came most naturally to her in that moment and wrapped her arms around him. Cody joined in as well, and they all started giggling at their silly group hug in the middle of the night.

"This was the worst day, but somehow being here with you guys made it so much better," Cody said without letting go.

"That's because Camp Sweet Clover people are the best people!" Melody said.

Cody scoffed. "Camp Sweet Clover. More like Camp Lost. Everyone here is so messed up!"

"Hey!" Melody said in mock-offence, and they all laughed again.

"Well, we should try to get some sleep," Tanner said.

"Yeah, I'm heading up to bed. I'll see you both in the morning," Melody said.

"I'm going to crash here, if that's okay," Cody said.

"Of course!" Tanner said as he climbed into bed. "Hit the light on the way out, would you, Melody?"

Melody watched Cody grab his Discman from the floor behind him and slide his headphones on. As she flipped the switch and closed the door, she faintly heard the tune of "Follow You Down" by Gin Blossoms. She climbed back up the stairs, wondering where Jack had been through all of this. *Surely he heard us?*

Something seemed off, but she pushed the train out of her mind, and climbed into bed and curled up under her covers. Melody hadn't yet closed her eyes when she heard a soft knock at the door.

"Yes?"

"It's Jack, can I come in?"

Melody sprang from her bed and opened the door. Before her stood a worn out looking Jack, dressed in a vintage green Sweet Clover t-shirt, grey track pants, and Birkenstocks.

"Hey."

"Hey, I've been wondering where you've been all night. We must have been keeping you up. My bad. Today's been such a mess..." Melody prattled on.

"It seemed like you and Tanner had it handled, so I didn't butt in. I wanted to check on you, though. You guys were working through things with Cody, and Tanner too, but I didn't hear anyone ask how you were doing. What you did today was so brave. You saved Piper's life. I don't even know if anyone has thanked you, but on behalf of everyone, thank you."

Melody blushed, like she always did when the attention was

on her. She was so averse to compliments. "I just did what anyone else would have done."

"In a perfect world, however, no one else could have fit through the ceiling beams. Or would have even thought to try! We would have had to knock down the door, and by then it might have been too late. How did you even come up with a plan for what to do before Raina got there?"

"Well, I'd like to blame it on a superb public school education, but it was just from watching TV. Those medical dramas get such a bad rap for being unrealistic, but I learn a lot, and today it proved worthwhile," Melody said.

"You're something, Melody Burton."

And at that, he pulled her in for a tight hug, then turned around and left the room without another word. Reaching the bottom of the stairs, he whispered goodnight into the dark, empty room, but she knew it was for her.

Melody's screams would have been deafening if anyone had been around to hear them. In front of her lay Piper's limp, pale body. Melody searched for a pulse in Piper's neck and wrist, then she knelt close to her chest, and not sensing any breath, started compressions, however, every time she pushed, more blood squeezed its way out of the cut on Piper's wrist.

Melody wondered how long she would pump Piper's chest before someone found them. An hour? Two? Til morning? Piper wouldn't survive that; she was losing too much blood. Melody pulled off her t-shirt and wrapped it around Piper's wrist. It soaked through instantly. Her methods weren't working.

A hospital monitor flatlined. Melody looked around, confused. *Aren't we at Sweet Clover? I thought we were in Piper's bedroom in the Fraser Bunkie? Wait, there aren't any monitors or any hospital equipment at all. What is happening?*

As Melody continued to do the compressions, the thick blood pooled around her bare feet. So much blood. With one more scream, Melody woke from the nightmare and sat straight up in bed drenched in sweat, her throat hoarse, like she'd been screaming aloud.

Her eyes darted around the room to make sure she was where she should be, and she collapsed back onto the bed and stared at the ceiling, wondering how a day that started so wonderfully ended up so tragic. Melody crawled out of bed just long enough to change into pyjamas that weren't soaked and cold, then returned to bed, pulled the covers over her head, and cried herself back to sleep.

CHAPTER 4
AUGUST 1994
MELODY

Melody woke to the sound of a dozen children outside her window attempting to play acoustic guitars, but it wasn't exactly music to her ears. She wasn't trying to be mean, just factual. So far, this proved to be the only downside to her private accommodations. If you weren't up in time for breakfast, you would wake to the chaos of the first session of the day. She groaned and crawled out of bed.

Glancing at her watch, Melody recounted the events of the last 24 hours. Waking up today, she was a different person than yesterday morning. Now, molasses-like thoughts filled her head, a thousand-pound weight burdened her body, and she struggled to open her eyes. So many negative inklings whirled around in her brain like a tornado. *Where is Piper? How is she? Why did this happen? How will Cody be today? Will I ever return to my old self, or am I forever changed?*

Melody was almost on the verge of tears before even putting on her Birks. She'd come to Sweet Clover looking for a fun week of tanning and helping with a project here or there. Now she wondered if the experience had completely traumatized her and if she would ever enjoy this place again. She worried her second home had become the source of nightmares instead, and shuddered as she recalled her screams in the night.

Melody had missed dinner and the pre-campfire snack the day before, so she knew that regardless of how nauseated she was, some breakfast and a little caffeine would likely help. She crept down the stairs, aware the guys might still be asleep after their late night. Melody weaved in and out of miniature guitar players, and across the middle of the camp to the dining hall.

Sneaking into the kitchen, she found one of her favourite cooks, Charlene, prepping lunch. Charlene let Melody into the fridge to find something to eat and asked how she'd slept. Melody managed a fake smile, and a mumbled, "Uh, okay, thanks."

After fixing herself some toast with peanut butter, Melody sauntered to the drink station for a giant mug of black coffee. She took both out the back door of the dining hall and walked down to the water for some peace, having forgotten that the day's first session had already started, and the lake was full of swimmers and kids canoeing. There would be no peace there.

Melody hiked back up the hill and instead found herself at Morningview Shores. All the benches were empty, and the water lapped onto the shore. The perfect place to enjoy her now lukewarm coffee and toast.

Sparkling under the morning sun, the lake looked so serene, and a gentle summer breeze drifted through the trees, wafting the faint scent of a nearby clover patch into Melody's vicinity. It never mattered how terrible her mood was; these surroundings always brought her comfort. While sitting with her thoughts, she heard someone walking up behind her, but didn't bother turning to see who it was, because she already sensed him.

Jack sat down on the bench beside her.

"How'd you sleep?"

This time, she gave an honest answer. "Terribly. I hope I didn't wake you…" she trailed off.

He didn't confirm or deny it, just threw his arm around her.

"I've got a surprise for you."

"Oh?" Melody said expectantly.

"We're not working today."

"We're not?"

Jack grinned at her. "No, we need some fun. Let's pack a picnic for lunch and take Cody and Tanner cliff jumping."

"Oh, sure, that sounds good," Melody agreed, hiding her disappointment that they would have company.

"Great!" Jack exclaimed with way too much energy for the lack of sleep they were both running on. "Meet me at noon in the bunkie," and he stood up and left without waiting for her to respond. She already recognized this as his MO, and it was so frustrating.

Melody was halfway through her coffee when she heard more footsteps behind her. Knowing it wouldn't be Jack again, she turned to look.

Leslie, the director, walked toward her with a face full of worry. Melody gave her a small smile and waited for her to sit.

"Morning, Melody. I wanted to check in. Nurse Raina told me you two had a productive discussion yesterday while sitting with Piper, and she shared how brave and strong you were. I didn't want to bombard you with more questions and forced conversation right away, so I let you rest. It's important that we talk now, though. Is that okay with you?"

Melody nodded. She figured she wasn't getting out of this, so she might as well get it over with.

"Great, thank you. How are you?"

"I feel like I got run over by a truck. I didn't sleep well, and I'm pretty worn out," Melody responded honestly.

Leslie's face knit with concern. "You should tell your parents what happened, Melody."

"Oh, let's not bother them now. Piper is okay and I'm okay. I've got friends here that need me, and I need them, and I don't want to worry my parents for nothing. Please, I'm really okay. I just need to relax for the day," Melody pleaded in her most grown-up sounding voice.

"Okay, if you're sure. I am going to be keeping a close eye on you, though. If I see anything of concern, I will call your mum right away."

"I understand. Really, I'm okay. Thanks for checking-in," Melody said before taking a sip of her coffee to punctuate the end of the conversation.

At noon, Melody sat at the bottom of the bunkie stairs, waiting for the guys. She had her flip-fops on, and her favourite bikini—black with a tiny daisy print—under her cut-off shorts. She topped the outfit with the Sweet Clover staff shirt she had swindled from the tuck shop that morning, despite only being a volunteer. It seemed fair, especially now, after everything she'd been through on her very first day.

Jack came out of his room and knocked on Tanner's door before heading to Melody and offering her a hand up.

"So chivalrous," Melody teased Jack, but he just winked at her.

Tanner exited his room, wearing a garish pair of teal and pink swim trunks with sunglasses and flamingos on them. Melody and Jack looked at each other and filled the room with friendly laughter.

"You said you're not out to everyone yet?" Melody questioned with a raised eyebrow.

Tanner laughed too.

"Right? How haven't my parents clued in by now?" he said, his blue eyes sparkling as he ran his fingers through his messy, natural red hair.

The three of them sauntered out onto the porch and looked around for Cody, but he was nowhere to be found. After waiting almost fifteen minutes, they left without him. The jumping rocks were a few minutes down a path through the forest. Melody had been plenty of times as a camper, but had never jumped. She never had the confidence.

In the short time she'd spent with these two, Melody gathered she wouldn't get away with not taking part, so she made the best of it. She started pulling her clothes off as she ran down the last stretch of path, ditched her flip-flops on the top of the rocks, and jumped before the guys had even caught up with her.

Melody crashed into the unseasonably cold water and a jolt of panic set in. The water was so frigid that her body instantly numbed with the shock of it. When she finally worked up the nerve to open her eyes in the dark blue lake, she saw the sun shining above, and relief washed over her as she kicked to the surface. Her head popped out of the water a little closer to the rocks than she should have, and she made a mental note to pay better attention next time.

Shielding her eyes from the sun, Melody gazed up at the top of the rocks. Tanner and Jack were there, clapping for her impromptu bravery—she was just full of surprises these days. Her face lit up with pride as she swam over to the makeshift steps worn in the cliff from years of wet feet clambering back up.

"Hey, is that a first for you, Melody Burton?" Jack asked.

"Yeah, I never got up the courage to jump before. Today it felt like I had nothing to lose."

"There's a badge for that!" Tanner shouted before she heard two splashes as the guys jumped in together.

Melody had never cared about the badge system at camp. She was already a senior camper when she started attending CSC, and all the other kids had wall banners covered in badges by then. It seemed silly for her to even attempt to catch up, so she never tried.

By the time she reached the top of the rocks, out of breath and heart still racing, the guys were right behind her. They all held hands at the top, Tanner, then Jack, then her. For a split second, Melody was sure she saw a glance exchanged between Tanner and Jack, but she shook it off and they all jumped together. Tanner screamed dramatically before they crashed into the water below and they kicked their way to the surface in unison.

Melody almost choked as she laughed at Tanner's shriek coming out of the water. Her body finally released the tension she'd been holding in her shoulders and jaw, and her nervous system relaxed for the first time since she left the boys' bathroom, as if she had cleansed herself of the previous day. She wondered how Jack knew this was exactly what she needed. After a few more jumps, each more daring than the last, Melody felt like she might be whole again. His small gesture was helping her heal.

The three friends spent the entire afternoon at the rocks, pausing between jumps only long enough to eat the picnic lunch Jack had wrangled up in the kitchen before meeting them. Ham and cheese sandwiches, apples, grapes, and salt and vinegar chips from the tuck shop. A perfect picnic lunch with just one missing piece.

"Did you bring any—" Melody started.

Jack pulled one last thing out of his bag before she could finish her sentence—fresh haystacks for dessert—which Melody had seen being prepared when she made her breakfast.

"Did someone tell you these are the way to my heart?"

Jack winked as Melody grabbed a haystack and laid down on her towel in the sliver of sun between the trees overhead. She closed her eyes and smiled.

Tanner groaned as he glimpsed the time on his watch. "I have a project to work on before dinner."

He packed up in the late afternoon sun, but Jack and Melody had nowhere to be, so they stayed at the rocks a little longer. Melody beamed, delighted to have this time alone with him, far from any urinals.

Now, with no buffer, tension lingered in the air. *Thanks Tanner.* Melody broke the silence with the first thing that came to mind. She ran and jumped off the cliff. This time, when she plunged into the cool water, instead of being hit with feelings of comfort, a wave of grief overcame her. By the time she emerged from the water, tears were streaming down her face. Luckily, from above, Jack couldn't tell the difference between tears and lake water, but he'd recognize the distinction soon enough.

Melody pulled herself up onto the ledge, and her body shook with sobs. She breathed deeply, willing it to stop.

"Are you hurt?" Jack called down to her when she didn't climb back up. He jumped in without hesitation.

Melody's panic rose, and by the time he reached her, she couldn't breathe. Her chest heaved as it fought against the perceived lack of air. Jack climbed onto the ledge beside her and cupped his hands around her face so she would look at him. Embarrassed, she tried to turn away.

"Watch me," he encouraged gently. He took slow, exaggerated breaths, offering for her to mimic him to calm her system.

Melody's breathing slowed, but the tears wouldn't stop. Jack held her, letting her finally come down from the day before. There was no tension in their silence this time. At last, when her tears dried and she stopped shaking, Melody looked up at Jack and whispered a hoarse, "Thank you."

This level of vulnerability caught her off guard, especially so soon after meeting someone, but Jack kept his arm around her while she composed herself.

"Are you ready to head back? It's almost time for dinner," Jack offered.

Melody's stomach was in knots after her emotional unraveling, but shame had crept in, and she wanted to put herself back together, so she didn't protest. Instead, she gave a slight nod, and Jack grabbed her hand and carefully pulled her up the cliff.

"I'm sorry about Piper. That must have been hard, and it seems like you're struggling with it. Maybe you should talk to someone?" Jack said.

"You're probably right."

"So, I'm here. You know where I live."

"Thank you," Melody said, but Jack shook his head as if to say it wasn't necessary, and laced his fingers between hers. They walked all the way back to camp hand in hand.

CHAPTER 5

AUGUST 1994
MELODY

Cody sat on the bunkie porch, his head resting on his arms, when Melody and Jack returned. Melody's ears picked up the faint sound of him sniffling through tears. Despite their shared experience in the night, she was currently a mess herself, so she left this one up to Jack. She quickly said, "Hey," and walked by them and up the stairs to her room.

Time for a shower to wash away the tears and lake water. She wanted to put herself together for once, to prove how okay she was, despite being anything but. At camp, people let a lot of things go, like frequent showering, and doing their hair and makeup. Wardrobes quickly became jean cut-offs and tees every single day, and there isn't a lot of effort involved in that look.

Melody heard Jack and Cody still talking on the porch as she came down the stairs with her things, so she popped out the back door instead, which no one used much anymore, and squeezed through the overgrown walkway and onto the main path. Melody debated whether to use the nearby dilapidated girls' bathroom, that your nose could find before your eyes did, or hike to the top of the hill to use the new, less-spidery girls' facilities. Deciding she already had enough of a workout today, she chose the closer of the two, wondering if she and Jack would be painting it next.

After a lukewarm shower, because there was never enough hot water at camp, Melody pretended to be a brand new girl. She put her hair into braided pigtails and threw on some coverup and mascara. Not a lot of work, but she looked a little less miserable. Something Melody would never admit to anyone here was how much she cared about her appearance. Back home, she never left her bedroom without makeup on, and she spent an excessive amount of time picking her clothes in the morning. Ironically, she didn't even fit into that stereotype at all. She typically dressed much more grunge than preppy, so it's not like she was trying to impress the popular guys at school.

After a mini existential crisis about why she even cared and what that said about her as a person, Melody walked back to the bunkie and found Cody and Jack still sitting on the porch. Cody hadn't moved, and Jack shrugged at her as she crept by with her things. Once inside, Melody breathed a sigh of relief. She was dealing with her own emotional rollercoaster right now, and she didn't have the energy for another Cody breakdown—she was on the verge of another one herself.

Melody slipped off her flip-flops and collapsed onto her bed. There were almost 20-minutes until the dinner bell, so she pulled out her journal, planning to work through some of her thoughts during that time. What came out wasn't a journal entry though, it was a letter to Piper.

> *August 21, 1994*
>
> *Piper,*
>
> *I'm not sure when or if you'll receive this letter. I don't know if I'll try to send it, if I can even figure out where you are, but it feels like the right thing to do, to write it.*

This place is a mess since you left. I'm not telling you that to hurt you, although I guess it will anyway, but I'm telling you hoping it will make you realize that so many people care about you and want you alive, and how negatively it would affect them if you were gone. What you did has changed so many of us.

Cody is having a literal breakdown. He doesn't have a clue where you are, he fears you're at home where your dad can hurt you, and he's also scared you're in a hospital where they're going to keep you locked away forever, or that you'll get out but you won't be the same, that the place will change you forever. He's probably right on the latter assumption.

I'm sorry that you were so lost and fed-up that you didn't want to live any longer. That must be terrifying, or maybe it's not, and that's why you decided what you did. I wish you talked to one of us before you took matters into your own hands. Me or Cody, we both would have been there for you. I guess it's difficult to spill your guts to someone, especially someone you aren't that close to. I'm sort of dealing with that now myself.

Finding you like I did, trying to save your life, has been eye-opening. Those moments somehow stole a piece of me that I'll never be able to get back. I don't want you to blame yourself. It seems like everyone else can speak openly and help each other process, and I just can't. So, it's making this difficult.

I heard you have had a hard life that must have brought you to this place, and it may look like I have this sunshiny perfect life, but I've been through hard things *too, and they've taken away my ability to share things with people. Jack is going out of his way to be there for me, trying to help me through this, but I'm all walls. So, I'm battling these demons on my own. My anxiety is worse than usual, and I'm having nightmares. I keep seeing you, and trying to save you, but in my dreams you don't survive.*

Piper, you need to survive. Is that too selfish of me to ask? Cody needs you. You can do this. We're all rooting for you.

Melody

Melody picked through her dinner, still not hungry and trapped in a pretty tumultuous headspace. She envisioned journaling as a helpful tool, however, when it turned into a letter to Piper, one she would never send, her anxiety crept sky high. She was on edge again and sick to her stomach. This trend was already exhausting, and she was over it.

Tanner came in late and slid in close to Melody on the bench, as if to convey that he was there for her. She leaned her head on his shoulder in appreciation and finally shoved a fork of mashed potatoes into her mouth.

"Girl, where have you been all day?" Tanner asked, blinking emphatically as if to feign ignorance.

Melody just gave him a side-eyed look.

Tanner smirked and took an exaggerated too-large bite of his food. Melody laughed out loud at his appalling table manners. She took another bite of potato. Tanner waited for her to be done chewing and made sure she was watching before he took another disgustingly large bite of chicken to encourage her.

Melody giggled, shaking her head, and soon her fog lifted. Her nagging thoughts floated away with each subsequent laugh, and in that moment, she felt overwhelmed with gratitude for Tanner.

Melody had little to say, but she listened as Tanner regaled her with story after story about the short time they hadn't spent together that afternoon. Despite all the tough things he'd talked about the night before, Tanner seemed unburdened. *Because of all the things he'd shared about, or despite?*

When he had run out of steam, he turned dramatically in his seat, leaned his chin on his hand and asked, "So, how was your date with Jack?"

Melody almost choked on her water. "My what?"

Tanner wiggled his eyebrows in a playful, all-knowing way and said nothing.

"That was so not a date! He's not into me like that," she said, trying to convince herself, but wanting it to be true. "He's three years older and headed off to college. No college guy wants anything to do with a high school girl. And wait, isn't that like… illegal?" she continued.

"Sure," Tanner said through a small smile, and took another bite of his dinner.

Melody tried to put his comments out of her mind, but of course, they were taking up all of her brain capacity now. She basked in the joy of this moment—free from obsessive thoughts about Piper.

Melody finished her dinner, but skipped the camp-wide game in favour of being alone in her room. She would catch up with everyone at the campfire.

A few minutes after sinking into the quiet of her bed, Melody heard the entire camp outside receiving their game instructions. By the sounds of it, they were playing capture the flag, an unfortunate choice because that would mean the campers would all be running right outside her room the entire time. She put her headphones on to drown out the noise and drifted into a daydream until a knock at the door startled her back to reality.

Jack.

"Come in!" Melody called.

Jack peeked his head around the wood door.

"Now if I didn't know better, I'd wonder if you had some ulterior motives coming up to my bedroom twice in 24 hours," Melody joked to convince Jack she was okay, despite it still being the furthest thing from the truth.

Jack laughed as he shut the door behind him, then he laid down on the bed beside her.

"Tanner said you seemed off at dinner."

"Really? He was so bubbly and enjoying his own world that I didn't assume he would have noticed much of anything."

Jack gently stared into her eyes like he could reach the darkest corners of her soul through them. "You are not okay."

Melody fought back the tear that tried to hurl itself down her cheek. "You're right. I am not okay. But I can't talk about not being okay. Or anything else. I am like an old envelope, sealed shut with 100-year-old saliva."

They looked at each other and laughed awkwardly at her analogy. The tear retreated.

"Okay, that sounded really wrong," Melody giggled.

"Well, I don't want to rip you open," Jack began, "so why don't you just try to tell me one small thing?"

He kindly kept up the charade of her terrible metaphor, so she figured she owed it to him.

"I am having a hard time. I'm having nightmares and keep seeing Piper's lifeless body. My stomach churns constantly, and I can't quiet my spiralling thoughts."

"See, that's a bunch of things! Thanks for sharing that with me. I am sorry you're dealing with so much, but based on what you've been going through, I'd assume it's normal and expected. You saw something horrible, you had to save someone's life.

That's probably going to mess you up for a while. Talk to a professional when you get home."

"It's hard enough talking to you. How will I talk to a stranger?"

"I'm a stranger," Jack said. "We've only known each other for what, a little over a day?"

"It feels like a lifetime," Melody said matter-of-factly.

The days passed quickly once the chaos settled. Melody spent her days working with Jack, hanging out with Tanner in the evenings, and consoling Cody in-between. She wasn't really doing well, but she was distracted enough with her group of guys, to cope. Cody on the other hand, was having a bit of a rougher time. On day three, Melody suggested he try writing a letter to Piper to process his feelings, like she had. Neither of them knew where she had gone, but they assumed they would find out eventually.

On day four, Leslie delivered Melody a letter addressed in unfamiliar penmanship. She wondered if it was what she had been waiting for, what she had been hoping would come before she left. She opened the envelope slowly. There was no return address, which was discouraging, but she hoped it would be in the letter somewhere.

August 22, 1994

Melody,

I suppose a thank you is in order, although I'm not sure I appreciate what you did. It is day two in the hospital, and this is the first time they've allowed me to have a pencil. Being here is like you're three years old and your parents don't let you out of their sight, even though everything hazardous is out of reach. At least, I assume that's what good parents do.

If I'm being honest, I'm pretty embarrassed about what I did. USC is the only place I ever felt safe, and now I took that away from myself, and others too. I didn't mean to hurt anyone. Sometimes I get so wrapped up in my fucked up brain, and once I spiral, there's no stopping it.

My brother getting hurt, while I wasn't there to protect him, was too much for me to handle. Regardless of our parents' situation or which foster home we lived in, he and I always looked out for each other. I always took care of him, and he always loved me. Sometimes he was the only one that loved me. So, if he wouldn't survive, I didn't want to either.

I'm not trying to make excuses for what I did, though I guess that's what it sounds like. Anyway, I wanted to tell you I'm sorry. Thanks for saving me. This time I think I mean it.

P.S. If you don't hate my guts and want to write back, my address is below.

Piper Shepard

Melody was glad Piper had included the address of her hospital in London. She grabbed the letter and ran off towards the boys' cabins, where she'd find Cody having the afternoon siesta with his campers.

"Cody!" she called into the wooded area, not knowing which cabin he stayed in.

"Yup?" a voice called from a distance. Cody jumped off a porch a few cabins back.

Melody waved the letter in the air and shouted, "I've got it!"

"Got what?" Cody called back, while a counsellor popped his head out of another cabin and shushed them both.

"She sent me a letter. I know where she is," Melody whispered as Cody got closer.

Cody stood immobile and Melody watched him take a few breaths. *He must be so relieved.* She gave him a moment to process before she said anything else. It was Cody who broke the silence.

"Why didn't she write to me? Why did she send you a letter? She barely even knows you!"

Uh oh. She needed to say something, anything.

"She was probably worried about disappointing you. Or it's possible she was afraid you wouldn't respond because of where she is right now," Melody responded.

"But why you?" Cody choked.

Melody tried not to take offence. "Sometimes it's easier to talk about hard things with people you aren't as close with. I don't know why, but it is. I've been learning that myself."

Cody said nothing.

"I'm sorry, Cody."

He grumbled something incoherent and walked away.

CHAPTER 6
AUGUST 1994
PIPER

Piper sat on the floor in the hospital hallway breathing heavily, shaking, and crying. She'd been there for at least ten minutes, when a nurse finally spotted her.

"You're okay, Piper. Come, let's take a nap."

She ushered Piper back into her room and gave her medication to help calm her.

Piper felt a deep sense of gratitude for the wave of relief as she laid on her side and let her nervous system calm, but she hated that the default reaction to every kind of emotion in this place was medication. The nurses were nice enough, but they never even asked what upset her. She had just dropped off a letter to be mailed to Melody, after hours of debating whether to send it, and now she was freaking out.

Will Melody get it in time before she left camp? Will she even open it? Will she use the address and write her back? Will she tell Cody? The thoughts ran through her head like they were on fire.

She needed more support. A friendly face, or at least a letter from someone who knew her. No one cared about her here. One more crazy on a floor full of crazies. At least that's the way she saw it.

Piper woke up from her drug-induced nap shortly before dinner and wandered down to the common room. The room was bleak. Beige walls, beige floors, small windows with grates over them to prevent escapes, a couple of grimy old couches in front of an even older television, and a few card tables and chairs for playing games or making art. The room smelled like it always did—a locker room of unwashed boys, hints of coffee, and bleach. *Yuck.*

She looked around for the only friend she'd made since being admitted, a girl named Nicki, who also found herself there because of a suicide attempt. Piper wasn't sure if it was smart to spend time with other people whose brains were as fucked up as hers, but it seemed to be her only option. Between their diagnoses and all the medications they were on, a lot of the other patients were practically catatonic, so there wasn't much opportunity for riveting conversation.

Spotting Nicki in the back corner, Piper shuffled over in her navy-blue hospital-issued slippers and sat down beside her.

"Hey, Nicki."

Nicki just looked at her and grunted.

"Rough day? Me too," Piper replied.

"They put me out this afternoon for screaming at a nurse who wanted to bathe me like a child. I told them I'd bathe when I was good and ready. That didn't go well."

Piper was at a loss for words, and that didn't happen very often.

"Anyway," Nicki continued, "I'm going to leave tomorrow. I'm sick of this place."

"How are you going to manage that?" Piper asked.

"I did my 72-hour hold and now I've been here an extra two weeks. Technically, I can leave whenever I want."

Piper had forgotten that Nicki was eighteen and therefore a legal adult. She could sign herself out and get back to her life.

Lucky. Piper was locked away until she convinced her grandma to retrieve her, and that might be tomorrow or a year from now. *It doesn't hurt to try, though,* a rogue thought hinted. In an instant, Piper decided to make that very desperate phone call the next day. She didn't want to be there anymore, and especially not without Nicki. She would be truly alone.

Sleep evaded Piper. Despite being on heavy medications to combat her insomnia, she tossed and turned all night. Apprehension about her plan for the morning stole her slumber. Piper kept going over it again and again in her mind.

1. *Call Grandma.*
2. *Explain to Grandma that they just keep drugging me and aren't helping me work on my problems, and that was supposed to be the point of being here.*
3. *Talk Grandma down when she comes up with all the reasons I need to stay here.*
4. *Convince Grandma to spring me from this joint ASAP.*

It was a pretty simple plan. Unless, of course, her grandma said no, or didn't even answer the phone. That would throw a wrench into her escape plan. *Minor detail, right? Plan B—maybe I could sneak out with Nicki?*

The darkness outside her barred window started turning purply pink as the sun rose. She'd hardly slept, and her body confirmed it. Piper's plan required her to be sharp, so with the list walked through thoroughly, she rolled over and closed her eyes again, with the hope of a snooze before breakfast.

Piper woke to the knock on her door. She had gotten about two hours of solid sleep, and her brain was processing a little more effectively.

Nicki waited for her at their usual table, and they ate breakfast together for the last time.

"I'm going home today!" Nicki whispered.

"I'm so happy for you," Piper said, faking excitement.

She didn't mention her plan to go home too, because she didn't want to steal Nicki's thunder. Breakfast was the usual cold mush of oatmeal and a banana. Piper didn't even like bananas. She noticed herself losing weight the longer she sat in this place. While most girls would love that, Piper had spent enough of her life emaciated, she didn't want to do that again. She had enough problems already, like her family.

Where would I even go home to? Grandma might let me stay in her house, but she is so conservative. Would we even survive it? I can't go back to my parents'—that will never be home again. I guess the last resort is foster care. It wouldn't be the first time. Would a foster home really be better than this place, though? At least no one will abuse me in the hospital. They just dope me up and leave me to my sorrows. Maybe this psych ward isn't so bad after all.

Realizing what she was thinking, Piper gave her head a shake and reminded herself that the hospital made her a prisoner. She needed out. She spent too much of the day talking to herself in her head like this. It was becoming a problem.

Piper asked to make her phone call right after breakfast. It rang four times before her grandma picked it up.

"Hello?"

"Grandma!" Piper said, trying to sound happy and healthy. "I'm ready to go home, Grandma. I am so much better, and I feel ready to get back to school and see my friends."

"Piper, the doctors haven't called me. They said they would call when you were ready to go."

"Grandma, the doctors barely see me, and the nurses just drug me up every chance they get and leave me in my room sleeping. It's not good here. They're not helping me."

"But you said you're better?" her grandma questioned.

"I mean, I am. The meds are helping. But I need to get out and see the sunshine and breathe fresh air, and talk to someone, a therapist, on my own, not in a group, to work through my stuff. They can't just medicate me and leave me to rot in this place. Please, Grandma. Come get me."

Piper was adept at turning it on when she needed to. After all, it took a lot of effort to survive a life like hers, a family like hers. She carefully walked on eggshells, saying and doing exactly what was necessary to placate her addict mom and avoid her dad's temper. Some might call it manipulation, but Piper called it smart.

"No," her grandma said, and hung up the phone.

Piper was stunned. Her grandma was her only option, and now there was no hope of getting out. Tears started collecting in the corners of her eyes, though she didn't want anyone to see them and give her more tranquilizers, so she ran to her room and sobbed in private.

Piper refused to give up. She desperately wanted to see Cody and get back to some semblance of a real life, so she kept trying. She and her grandma repeated the same song and dance for three days in a row until the fourth day, when something finally changed.

"Fine," her grandma said, "put one of the staff on the phone."

Piper shouted for a nurse, but no one came.

"Hold on Grandma, let me find someone."

By the time Piper got back to the phone with a nurse, her grandma had hung up. *You'd think a nurse would be easier to find in a hospital. Weren't they supposed to be monitoring the patients?* Piper dialled again.

"Grandma, I have the nurse here."

"Yes, hello. I am coming to sign Piper out today. Please help her pack her things," her grandma said bluntly, as though they may protest, so she had to speak with such confidence. Grandma was skilled in getting what she wanted too.

"Yes, ma'am," the nurse replied and hung up the phone.

She'd done it. She was getting out of here. Piper skipped back to her room and floated around with excitement as she gathered her things. She would call Cody right away and patch things up. Piper had been missing him so much, and she hoped he missed her too.

That afternoon, a nurse escorted Piper and her grandma out of the psychiatric ward, and they weaved their way through the rest of the hospital corridors to the front entrance in silence. As soon as the automatic doors opened for them, Piper felt the sun and an early-autumn breeze on her face for the first time in weeks. She took a deep breath and exhaled all her worries before sprinting to the payphone at the corner of the parking lot.

"Piper?" her grandma shouted after her.

Piper didn't reply. She picked up the receiver and put in Cody's number. She had spent her entire stay staring at the piece of paper he had written it on and given to her the first day they met.

"Hello?" Cody said.

"Cody! I'm so glad I got you! I'm going home!" Piper squirmed with joy.

"Oh?" he questioned, monotone.

Piper leaned against the side of the payphone. "Yes, I got released today. I miss you so much. Can we can see each other soon?"

"Oh, I'm not sure Piper. Weren't you supposed to be in the hospital for at least a month? Isn't that what you told Melody in your letter?"

"Yes, but that place wasn't good for me. My grandma signed me out today."

"Piper, that's not a good idea. I mean, you tried to take your life. At camp. You really messed up so many of us, don't you get that? You aren't magically better after, like, two weeks."

Piper's body deflated. "I get that, Cody, and I feel bad about it. I'm going to see a therapist, though, and I'm on meds. I'm taking care of it, okay? And I want to see you," Piper spewed manically.

"Piper, you didn't even write me, you wrote to Melody. I kind of thought you were done with me. We also live almost five hours apart, and only one of us drives. How are we going to see each other? Besides, school starts in a few days and I need to get ready for that. I don't think we'll be able to see each other for a while."

Piper's heart dropped as she sat in the awkward silence between them. Cody spoke first.

"Piper, I'm sorry. It might be best if we don't date right now. You need to get better, and I am not ready for all of ...this." He trailed off. "I mean, I spent the last session at camp an emotional wreck, worrying about you. Now here you are casually asking to hang out. I need time, and you need help. You also need to fix things with Melody. She's got like PTSD or something from saving your life. She is pretty messed up, although she's trying to hide it from everyone."

Piper hadn't considered how Melody would feel since she'd written her the letter. She'd only been worried about how scared Cody must have been as her boyfriend. But Melody saw some scary stuff, and that would take a toll on her. Everything came into focus for Piper for the first time. She realized she did, in fact, need help. She had been so wrapped up in her own perspective, she hadn't even stopped to consider what her friends might deal with in the aftermath. *Selfish.*

"Cody, I'm sorry, I truly am. I'm going to fix things with Melody and you, okay?"

Cody stayed silent.

"Cody, please, I need you!" Piper leaned her head against the phone in defeat.

"I'm sorry too. But you don't need me, you need help that I can't give. I have to go." Cody hung up.

It was like someone had punched Piper in the gut and knocked the wind out of her. Her heart changed from a hopeful steady beat to fearful thundering. *Was he right? Had all of this been a terrible mistake?*

Her grandma had been waiting in the car pulled up at the curb, but after seeing Piper's visceral reaction, rolled down the window and called for her to get in.

"Piper, you really don't seem okay. We should take you back."

"No, Grandma, my boyfriend just broke up with me. I'm not crazy, I'm sad."

"I wish you'd stop using that word. It must not make you feel very good about yourself. Come on, let's go get something to eat. You look like you need to put some meat back on your bones."

"Okay, Grandma," Piper said through silent tears running down her cheeks.

CHAPTER 7
SEPTEMBER 1994
PIPER

Piper spent three days settling in at her grandma's, most of which was in bed mourning her relationship with Cody, before she felt ready to call Melody. It wasn't until she'd made the decision, however, that she realized she didn't have Melody's phone number, or even her address. All Piper had to go on was her family lived in Whitby. She called Information and asked for the Burtons in Whitby, Ontario. There were twelve to choose from. She had no way of narrowing the list down, and calling all twelve felt daunting, so she mustered up all the courage in her bones to call Cody again.

"Cody, I'm sorry to call you. I am respecting your wishes, I promise, but I'm trying to get in touch with Melody to apologize, like I said I would. But I guess I didn't get her phone number or address. Do you have it?"

"No, but Tanner does. I can call him and ask for it."

"Oh, thank you, Cody, you're the best," Piper said, her voice dripping sweet like honey, hoping he'd have missed her enough to keep talking.

"Sure. I'll call you back," Cody said and hung up the phone.

Piper sat by the phone and waited and waited. Thirty minutes passed by before she realized he would not call right back, so instead she planned to go for a walk into town for a much-needed change of scenery. Her grandma caught her just as she was heading out the door.

"It's not safe for you to go by yourself."

"Grandma…" Piper whined, "I can walk to town. It's like ten minutes."

"Maybe so," said her grandma, "however, it's not the walk I'm worried about. It's you being alone. If you want to go to town, I will drive you. Don't forget you have a psychiatry appointment at five, though."

How could I forget? Piper had been dreading the appointment since her grandma made it the day she got home from the hospital. She'd never been to a psychiatrist before, other than speaking with some at the hospital, which was mostly in group settings. She figured the experience would be about as enjoyable as the dentist.

"Fine, you can drive me. I want to go get a coffee that doesn't suck and pickup postage stamps for some letters to friends," Piper explained.

"Very well," her grandma replied, not even chastising her coffee insult.

They got to town and home again within 30 minutes, but Piper had, of course, missed Cody's call during that time. He left a message on the machine with Melody's address, but no phone number. Piper wondered if that was on purpose, and whether Tanner or Cody had decided not to share it with her. *It doesn't matter.* She sat down and addressed the envelope, glad that she's picked up stamps.

Piper still had to write the letter. That would be the hard part, and she wasn't quite ready to do it yet. It was almost time for her appointment, anyway. She tried to call Cody back and thank him before she had to leave, and it surprised her when he answered.

"Hello?"

"Hey, it's Piper."

"Oh, hey. I left a message with Melody's address for you," Cody said.

"Yeah, that's what I was calling about. I wanted to thank you. And also, did you get her phone number or just her address?" Piper asked.

"Just her address. Tanner wasn't sure if he should give out her phone number without her permission," he explained.

"Oh, so not that you didn't want to give it to me?"

"Piper, I don't know what you're trying to do, but I already did you a favour by getting her address. You can't keep calling me. This isn't respecting my decision for us to be apart. I need to focus on school, so please stop calling."

"Are you sure it's about school and long distance, and not about me being crazy?" Piper spat back.

"Does it matter?" Cody asked.

"Yes!" Piper shouted.

"Fine. Things were fun between us at camp. But we're not at camp now. You hurt so many people, me included, and you have a lot of problems to sort out. That's not good for me right now. This isn't fun anymore. I can't be what you need."

"Cody, I'm headed to the psychiatrist in, like, half an hour, to get help," Piper said.

"That's great. Good luck with that," Cody said before the phone went dead.

Piper's breath hitched. *He broke up with me because of my mental health problems? Does he not see I am getting help and trying to be better? That I want to be better for him?* Piper crumpled to the floor. She was busy trying to shove her despair back inside her guts where it belonged when her grandma interrupted her.

"Come on, Piper, time to go!" she called up the stairs.

He didn't want me. I am broken. I wasn't good enough for him and I will never be good enough for anyone. What is the point, anyway?

"Piper!" her grandma called again.

Piper grabbed her bag and stomped down the stairs.

"I'm here Grandma, let's go," Piper said as she wiped the last of her tears from her cheeks.

She slid into the passenger seat and gave her grandma a half-hearted smile. Her grandma smiled back and stared at Piper's puffy red eyes, but she never said a word. Piper almost wished she would say something. It might have made the moment feel more real.

CHAPTER 8
SEPTEMBER 1994
MELODY

Melody now spent most of her time listening to the CDs she'd bought, featuring all the songs that reminded her of camp. She also journaled every day, trying to work out the nightmares she was still having. She hadn't sent letters to the guys yet because she didn't want to seem too eager. Outside daydreaming about camp, she spent her time getting ready for school to start. Her mum had taken her shopping at Biway for the supplies she needed, and she'd bought a fresh pair of Converse with the allowance money she'd saved all summer.

"Melody, I have to be honest. I'm a little worried about you," her mum said in the middle of the shoe aisle.

"Mum, I'm fine."

"You're not. You don't think after fifteen years I can read my baby? You are not fine. You haven't been fine since you came home. What happened at camp?"

"I had a lot of fun! I made some great friends. There was some drama, and yes, a friend got hurt and had to go home, but it's not worth talking about. I'm okay," Melody said.

Her mum let it go, for the time being.

After a few days of boring herself to death, Melody called

Kalliope to hang out. Melody was sure she might burst if she didn't tell someone the story and the trauma they'd all experienced. Kali may not have been at camp this time around, but she at least was familiar with the camp experience, and would get it.

Leslie had urged Melody to tell her parents everything when she returned home, explaining she feared for Melody's mental health, and rightfully so. Of course, Melody didn't. For confidentiality reasons, Leslie could not personally share the exact details with Melody's parents, so they were still in the dark. Melody knew if she explained the gruesome story to her parents, they would never let her go back to camp to work or visit.

Kalliope, of course, accepted the invitation for a dish session, and Melody's mum, thrilled she was going out and doing something with an old friend, offered to drive her for the visit. Melody unleashed her story on Kali without so much as a "hello", and she sat with her jaw on the floor for the entire tale.

"So, I guess I saved her life, but it kinda screwed up mine. Now I'm dealing with nightmares and my anxiety is so bad. Mum is asking questions, but I'm afraid of what she'll do if she finds out. She'll think I'm crazy or something," Melody finished.

"Well, mental illness isn't contagious."

"Duh," Melody replied with an eye-roll, "but that doesn't mean she won't send me to therapy, or even worse, never let me go back to CSC."

"Wouldn't therapy be good for you, though? I mean, having nightmares and being anxious all the time isn't a healthy way to live, Melody."

"Who even goes to therapy, though? Isn't that only for crazy people?"

"Me. I go to therapy," Kalliope said with a huff and turned away from Melody.

"Oh, my bad! Kali, you never told me. I didn't mean it."

"You have been so preoccupied with camp, for weeks before

you left, and since you've been home, you've been a ghost. You haven't once asked me how I've been doing this summer. When would I have had the time to tell you?"

"I've been a pretty shitty friend," Melody said to the ground.

"You've been a pretty shitty friend."

"I'm going to do better," Melody said, meeting Kali's eyes.

"And you're going to go to therapy?"

"Well, let's not get ahead of ourselves!" Melody joked.

Both girls dissolved into giggles. The visit was brief, but Melody had unburdened herself, which was exactly what she needed.

Melody returned home to a message from Tanner on her machine.

"Hey girl, hey!" it began in his goofy drawl. "I've got lots to dish, so call me back when you get a minute, okay? I don't want to leave it all here on your machine. Call me!"

Melody picked up the phone and dialled Tanner's number. It only rang once before someone answered.

"Hel—" the sound squeaked out, and the person cleared their voice and tried again, "Hello?" they asked much deeper this time.

"Hi, it's Melody, I'm—"

"Oh hey, girl!" Tanner cut her off, using his natural voice this time.

She laughed out loud. "Hey! I wasn't sure if it was you."

"You mean the switch from my natural voice to my straight voice didn't give me away?"

Melody sensed Tanner was grinning just by his tone. It was nice that she already knew him well enough to sense those types of things over the phone.

"Okay, so here's the update. You ready?" He didn't wait for her to respond. "So Piper called Cody the other day, saying she was out of the hospital and wanted to see him. That wasn't good for either of them, so he broke up with her, like, the minute she walked out of the hospital. Bold, right? Then she calls him a few days later, the audacity, and asks for your phone number and address. Cody didn't have them, so he called me. But I was wondering, would Miss Melody want me sharing her phone number with this girl who, like, totally made a mess of everything at camp? I think not. I figured the address was fine though, because you'd have the choice to just not open the letters if you didn't want to read them, right? So, I gave Cody your address, and told him to tell Piper that I didn't have your phone number, because, well, I don't want any of us blamed for not giving it to her, right? So Cody calls her and leaves the information on her answering machine, and then she calls him back! Why, Piper? Leave this poor man alone! Anyway, he basically tells her to get lost, and I wish he'd been a little nicer, but you have seen how quickly Cody's emotions get the best of him. So then he hangs up on her! Of course, Cody calls me to tell me what happened. Anyway, that's the 4-1-1, girl."

Melody giggled as she hung on every word of Tanner's story. She had missed him. He somehow seemed even more exuberant than he was before. *Kind of impressive for Tanner. Had he come out to his parents when he got home?*

She didn't care that he'd given out her address, but she was damn glad he hadn't given out her phone number. Melody wanted time to consider anything Piper said, and to not have to respond right away during a phone call. It's likely that she was having a tough time, but Melody was still trying to process her own stuff since she got home. Besides, being on the phone still sent her into a panic on a good day—though not with Tanner apparently—let alone with a triggering conversation from the other end.

"You are quite the storyteller, my friend," Melody said when Tanner stopped for air. "Thanks for not giving Cody my phone number. I mean, he should have it, but it's better Piper doesn't, for now. It's fine that she has my address, though. You did the right thing."

Tanner heaved an exaggerated sigh of relief. "Perfection. So, what's new?"

"Well, I still haven't told my parents about what happened at camp. My mum can sense something is off, but I don't want to deal with any more fallout. My friend, Kali, thinks I need therapy. I guess I'll just see how things go for now."

Tanner switched into his serious mode. "I mean, therapy is never a bad idea. But I get why you don't want to tell your parents. I'm here if you need to chat."

"Thanks, Tanner. I had a pretty exhausting day, so I'm going to let you go here, but I'll talk to you soon, okay?"

"Okie, catch you on the flip side," Tanner said, and the phone went dead.

Bye, I guess? What is with these camp boys and always getting the last word in, or ducking out of conversations in a split second? Melody rolled her eyes and smirked.

The emotional retelling of the events at Camp Sweet Clover, and Tanner's exuberant monologue, had left Melody drained. She crawled into bed and hit play on the VCR. The opening credits of "The Breakfast Club" began, because what else would she choose?

CHAPTER 9
SEPTEMBER 1994
MELODY

The last days of summer vacation flew by, and Melody spent her time preparing to be back in her high school halls, and dreading every minute of the day. She thought about Jack constantly, but the idea of hearing his voice and then missing him even more filled her with such dread that she avoided calling to catch-up. She had sent him a letter in the hopes it would reach him before he left for school though, as the universities started a week later than the secondary schools.

September 4, 1994

Jack,

It's been over a week, and I am still struggling to get back to normal life. I miss Sweet Clover so much. The pine-scented air, the campfire sing-alongs, the joy of finding baked oatmeal on the table for breakfast, and you and Tanner—but mostly you. Once I get back to school on Tuesday, I hope I'll be okay again, but as of right now, I am kind of a mess.

Are you excited about starting college? You must be nervous. Don't forget to give me your new address. Awkward number of letters incoming. Just kidding! Hopefully, I can come visit you sometime? I mean, it's only like an hour and a half, right? There are busses, and I will get my license soon.

I've been listening to our songs a lot. My Discman keeps skipping every time I float around my room to Wildflowers. Something about it reminds me of CSC so much. What have you been up to since you got home? Packing, I guess? Are you scared to be moving out for the first time? I don't think I will be, though I'm sure some people are.

Have you heard anything from Tanner or Cody? I've been talking to Tanner a bit. He sounds good, happy. I hope he's going to have a better year at school. It seemed like you two hit it off this summer... are you keeping secrets from me, Jack?

Anyway, I should go. I need to get my bag packed and ready so I can enjoy my last day of summer tomorrow. School, yay. Talk to you soon, I hope.

Melody

School didn't recreate Melody's pre-camp life as much as she would have liked. Her school friends still resented her for being unreliable that summer, like Kali had, and Melody still hadn't come to terms with being home. It didn't help that the nightmares still plagued her every night, so she was drastically sleep deprived. School and friend drama are hard enough with full mental faculties, but when you've only accumulated fifteen hours of sleep in the past four days, it makes it even harder.

Worse still, Melody's parents wouldn't let up with their questions. When she walked in the door after her first day of school, there was no cheerful banter and asking about teachers. Melody's mum told her to sit down and explained she'd made an appointment with a therapist for her, because something was clearly going on.

"I don't need a therapist, Mum!" Melody argued.

"Melody, I've asked you multiple times to talk to me, to tell me what happened at camp, to explain why you're locked in your room all the time with your headphones on, and why you're having nightmares? You're not acting like yourself."

"I miss my friends. I miss camp. That's all."

"It seems like it's more than that, and if you don't want to talk to me, that's fine, but you need to talk to someone. Your appointment is Friday after school."

Melody sighed and stomped up the stairs. She sensed her mum watching her every step and wanted to get to her room and shut the door for some privacy. *I guess Kali will get her wish after all.*

Melody's mum picked her up from school on Friday and drove straight to the appointment. Melody's agitation increased throughout the drive; she tapped her feet and drummed her fingers to release it. Cars were driving too close. Her clothing itched. *Why is it so damn hot in here?*

Melody checked in with a way-too-perky receptionist at the front desk and sat in an uncomfortable 70s looking moss-green wool chair waiting her turn. Glancing around the office, she noticed all the magazines on the tables were of non-confrontational topics like gardening, home design, and crafting. Not only that, but they were all at least two years old. It didn't give her much faith for the type of person she was going to meet down the hall.

"Ms. Burton?" the receptionist called, "Dr. Clark will see you now."

Dr. Clark. Melody pictured an old white man with glasses halfway down his nose and a leather notebook in his hand. When she opened the door at the end of the hall, however, she was pleased to see a young Black woman instead.

"Hi Melody, I'm Dr. Clark, please have a seat."

Her voice dripped like honey, warm and friendly; the voice teachers use on the first day of school when everything is shiny and new.

"What brings you in today?" Dr. Clark asked as Melody stared at the floor, fidgeting with her rings.

She was wearing her favourite pink high-top Converse. One always untied itself, so she busied herself with retying it.

"My mum made this appointment for me. She said I'm not acting myself. I don't need to be here though, I'm not crazy."

"Well, first Melody, we don't like the word crazy here. It has a negative connotation and mental illness doesn't need any help with that."

"Mental illness?" Melody practically shrieked. "I'm not mentally ill."

"I didn't mean to imply that, Melody. However, your mum mentioned some things when she called that had her concerned, and we want to understand, that's all."

"Okay," Melody said, picking at the hole in her jeans.

"Why don't you tell me a bit about your summer?" Dr. Clark asked.

Melody paused before replying, wondering where she would even begin. Dr. Clark watched her, and as if she read Melody's mind, said, "Start at the beginning."

Melody returned home from her therapy appointment to find a letter waiting for her in the kitchen. She dropped her backpack with a thud and snatched the letter off the counter, hoping it was from Jack. The return address was from London though, not Hamilton. *Piper.* Even though Melody expected one, it still caught her by surprise, and she hesitated to open it.

"Who's it from?" her mum asked, coming in behind her.

"Uh, a friend from camp. I've got homework to do. I'm going upstairs." Melody picked up her backpack again and thundered up the stairs.

Throwing herself down on the bed, she peeled the envelope open, being careful not to tear the return address, as it differed from the hospital address on the first letter. Before she'd even unfolded it, the chaotic nature of the letter hit her like a brick wall. Something was off, and she felt terrified to read it.

September 6, 1994,

Melody,

I'm home from the hospital now. I left after two weeks, because I couldn't take it anymore. I didn't need to be there, anyway. They were drugging me up and forcing me to stay in my room all the time, and how is that going to help me? Besides, I'm good now.

I had to call Cody to get your address, and he got it from Tanner. I hope you're not mad. But I needed to talk to you. I mean, Cody said I should apologize, so I guess that's what I'm doing.

Is that what you're doing? Melody felt herself bubble up with anger, like a cartoon character turning red before they blow steam out their ears.

It's that sometimes my thoughts get so jumbled in my head and it makes me like hyper or something. And other times, my brain freezes, paralyzing me. It's pretty crazy honestly, well I'm pretty crazy I guess, but that place was only making me worse.

Stuff isn't great here either, though. My grandma is so overprotective, and my few friends somehow heard rumours they had committed me, so they are all avoiding me like the plague, like craziness is contagious or something. Isn't that stupid?

Ironically, Melody deduced that in this case, it seemed like craziness was contagious. *Oh, not craziness. I'm not supposed to use that word anymore.* Piper's mental illness and subsequent suicide attempt had caused Melody to develop PTSD. At least that's what her therapist hypothesized. *So doesn't that kind of make it contagious somehow?*

Anyway, Cody seems to be done with me and I've hurt you too, so I just wanted to write you this and say I'm sorry, and that you'll never have to worry about seeing me or hearing from

me again. I hope I haven't caused you too
much trouble.

    Piper

That's it? That ending dripped with ominous undertones. What did Piper mean about not bothering me anymore? Was this a goodbye letter? Like the ultimate goodbye? She hadn't left a note the first time, so it made little sense that she'd leave one now, right?

Melody's head spun. Terror crept in, and she couldn't stand to be alone with this information. Without hesitating, she called Cody.

"Cody?" Melody blurted into the receiver. "Cody. I think Piper is going to hurt herself again. What do we do? Should we call 911? Or her grandma?"

"Melody, what are you talking about?" Cody asked.

"I got a letter from Piper and she sounded, well, not good."

"Melody, she would have written that letter days ago. If that was really her intention, it would already be too late!" Melody heard the panic rising in Cody's voice.

"I know."

"I'm going to call her and see if I can talk to her," Cody said. "Let me call you back."

Relieved by that idea, Melody hung up. *How would that conversation go? Or what if... what if there wouldn't be a conversation because Piper was already gone? Maybe I should have called the police.* She paced back and forth in her room until the phone rang.

"Melody," Cody said, his tone tense with fear, "her grandma wouldn't let her come to the phone. She said she had given her bad news about her brother, and it wasn't a good time. I didn't want to worry her, so I said nothing. I mean, obviously Piper is still alive and everything, but her brother is the most important person to her. That news set her off before the first time, so now I'm really worried. I can't explain it, but maybe we should go there. I had kind of written her off, but the thought of never seeing or speaking to her again makes me sick. I can't shake the feeling that I need to do this. Can I come get you?"

Melody struggled to process his suggestion. Cody wanted to pick her up and drive to Piper's? She lived in London, almost three hours away, and it was already six o'clock.

"Um, I'll ask, although my mother will surely disapprove of my driving across the province with a boy she's never met. That doesn't sound sketchy at all! What if we make it more of a group thing? We can call Jack and Tanner?"

"Okay, but let's make it quick. This is urgent," Cody pleaded.

"Okay, you call Tanner, I'll call Jack, and then call me back," Melody said. Having a task to accomplish was always calming for her, despite being terrified of speaking with Jack on the phone.

"You should call and talk to her grandma, though," Cody suggested.

"If I do that, she might be back in the hospital before we even get there," Melody replied.

"Wouldn't that be better?" Cody wondered aloud.

"You're the expert, this was your idea!" Melody hissed.

Cody sighed. "Just call Jack, I guess."

Melody hung up and dialled Jack's number. She'd only been home for a week, but she already had it memorized, just in case. Jack would be moving to college soon; however, she hoped he'd have time for a little Friday night road trip first.

"Hello?" Jack said.

"Jack? It's Melody. There's an emergency, sort of. Piper is in a bad way and Cody wants to drive out there, but my mum won't let me go with some strange boy, and we hoped if you and Tanner came, it would be better? You're so calm under pressure. Um, but, we want to go like right now."

"Melody, I'm moving to college on Sunday. This is kind of terrible timing. And why would driving to London with three strange boys be better than one? It sounds crazy."

"Yeah, that's the word of the day," Melody couldn't help but joke. "Will you come?"

"I mean, I guess if you guys need me. I can't really say no now. What if something happened because I didn't come? Let me pack my stuff. I'll drive down to your place and we can wait for Cody there."

"Okay, thanks, I'll see you soon."

Jack had an hour's drive to get to Melody's, but Cody had about an hour and a half, so the timing fit. Tanner lived about halfway between Melody and Piper, so he was a quick stop along the way. The only thing left to figure out was what Melody would tell her mum about this spontaneous adventure.

"Mum?" she called as she walked down the stairs. "Are you home?"

"Yes?" her mum called from the kitchen.

"Mum. I have something to tell you, and I don't want you to get upset, but I have to do this. One of our friends from camp is in trouble, and Cody and Jack want to come pick me up and we're going to drive out to London, and pick Tanner up on the way, and go try to help this friend. We'll be gone overnight. Please don't be mad, they're already on their way," Melody rambled, glossing over key details her mum would want to be privy to.

"Melody Lennon Burton. How dare you spring this on me!" she roared. Melody winced.

"I'm sorry, Mum. It's so last minute, we just planned this. But it's important. Please let me go," Melody begged.

"Well, they're already on their way, so how can I say no? However, I expect a full explanation of all this strange behaviour when you get home."

"Oh, thank you! I will," Melody promised, as relief flooded over her, though she hoped her mum would forget about that promise by the time she returned.

Melody retreated to her room to pack her bag and freshen up before Jack arrived. This trip was not about her, but being enclosed in a car with three guys for many hours at least required some deodorant and minty breath.

The three of them were on the road before eight o'clock, and the air in the sedan weighed heavy and thick with tension. Melody assumed they'd all be hanging out again, but under much different circumstances. Jack had given her the front seat, so she begrudgingly sat with Cody, but planned to swap when they stopped at Tanner's house. It was going to be a long night.

CHAPTER 10
SEPTEMBER 1994
MELODY

The friends arrived at Tanner's just after nine o'clock and still had over an hour to go. Cody, Melody, and Jack all got out of the car to stretch their legs. Judging by the groans and creaks that came out of them, you'd think they were at least two decades older. Tanner came bopping down the driveway, way too excited for the weight of the situation.

"Ahoy, friends!" he exclaimed with a smile.

"Ah, yes, 'ahoy'. The standard greeting when embarking on a road trip to save an acquaintance from cutting their timeline short," Jack responded. The friends all chuckled despite the implication of impending doom.

Melody climbed into the backseat, hoping Jack would slide in beside her, and he did. Tanner sat up front with Cody.

The gravity of the situation descended on the group once again. Despite their exhaustion from the drive, and the late hour, the nerves and adrenaline kept them wired. Their conversations bubbled in fits and starts.

What Melody had welcomed as a chance to spend a significant amount of time with Jack turned out to be a more of a damper on their budding friendship. A dark cloud seemed to hang over Jack, threatening to burst, and coupled with Melody's anxiety about what would come next, it created a poor combination. She choked on her words, struggling to say anything of substance, and Jack, who was usually super chatty, just stared out the window. Melody wondered if she'd made a huge mistake.

"Cody," she said towards the front seat. "Are we doing this all wrong? Should we have called the police and let them handle it?"

"Probably," Cody said, visibly drained.

Tanner looked over his shoulder at her and shrugged.

Melody took the opportunity to change the subject. "Hey Tanner, you sounded pretty happy on the phone, before all this. Are things going well at home?"

"Yeah, I didn't want to bring it up right now because it seemed insensitive, but things are really great. I came out to my parents!"

The whole car started cheering, and the mood lifted instantly. A chorus of congratulatory sentiments fought for airtime, and Tanner beamed.

"Thanks guys, the enormous weight on my shoulders has lifted. I'm free, and I can be the guy I've been hiding, anywhere and everywhere. I kind of want to shout it from the rooftops."

"So, your parents were cool?" Jack asked, his eyes wide.

"They were amazing. You won't believe what they said—'we know.' They'd suspected it since I was about four years old, and they were waiting for me to be ready to bring it up on my own. I am so lucky."

"Wow, that's incredible," Jack said. "I wish my parents were like that."

Melody shot Jack a glance across the backseat that she hoped would translate as, "What the hell?", but Jack didn't elaborate.

Tanner shared the rest of the experience; after telling his parents, he told his sister, who reacted as if his news was incredibly unsurprising and underwhelming. It made Melody so happy that everything worked out for him and he was embracing his authentic self. She couldn't imagine what it was like to keep such an important, life-changing secret like that, but it must have been a gift that he didn't have to carry it anymore.

"Next exit, London," Cody announced from behind the wheel.

They were almost there, and Melody's elation quickly vanished as her heart rate jumped and her stomach tied itself in knots. She doubted herself all over again. *What if we get there and Piper is already gone? What if I find her again, but this time, I can't save her? What if I read way too much into the letter and that's not what Piper meant at all, and she is fine? What if…*

At just after ten o'clock they pulled into Piper's driveway. There were no first responder vehicles outside. *What a relief! How are we going to get into the house without Piper's grandma waking up, though?* No one had been to this house before, so they weren't sure which window would be Piper's. Jack had the smart idea of looking for the one with the light on as it wasn't likely Piper would be asleep at this hour.

The group crept around the house, through the chainlink gate to the backyard, and found a room with a light on. They took turns throwing small pebbles at the window, and Melody, with her many years on a baseball diamond, made contact first. If it hadn't been dark, Melody guessed she might have spotted pink cheeks from Cody, their token jock. They stood still and watched, but nothing happened.

Melody threw another pebble and this time, the person in the room heard it. A shadow slinked to the window, likely scared of what they would find below. Melody worried if the right person would appear in the glass. The group were in the dark below, making it impossible to see their faces, and the backlit person in the window was indistinguishable from their side too. Jack, being

Jack, had a flashlight on his key chain, so he shone it at Cody's face, and the upstairs figure started jumping up and down. *Success.*

The person raised a finger to say "one minute", and disappeared from view. A few seconds later, Piper came sprinting out of the patio doors and into Cody's arms. She pulled back and grew wide-eyed with surprise as she saw the other three faces beside him.

Piper seemed perfectly okay. Jack's half-smile alluded to the fact that she looked good. Tanner, having more experiences similar to Piper's, wore an expression that wasn't as relieved as the other two. His eyebrows furrowed and his mouth bordered on frowning instead of smiling. They all breathed a collective sigh of relief, however, when it sunk in that she was still alive. It felt like hours before someone spoke.

"What are you all doing here?" Piper shrieked at a whispered volume.

"You worried us," Cody said. "Melody said she got a letter from you and it seemed kind of… off. She thought you might be a danger to yourself. She rounded us all up to come and make sure you are okay."

"I am now," Piper sighed. "Thank you so much, Melody."

"Piper, was I right about your letter? Were you going to hurt yourself again? I didn't want to call the police in case I was wrong. It's hard to read tones in letters sometimes."

"Well, uh, I…" Piper pulled at her hoodie sleeve as she trailed off.

Melody had been right, after all. She wasn't sure to what extent, however, as Piper was avoiding incriminating herself. Melody hadn't wanted to freak out for no reason but her gut was right, though it terrified her she had been right. *What if I had ignored my instincts? What if we hadn't come? What if we'd been too late and I should have just called the cops? What if…*

Relief turned to anger, washing over Melody like hot lava. She didn't direct her anger at Piper; she inflicted it on herself. Melody backed away from the group and found a patio chair to crumple into. She didn't expect the group to follow her. In fact, she had been trying to get away from them, but they did anyway.

"Melody, you saved me again," Piper said.

Tanner opened his mouth as if to speak, but changed his mind. Jack seized the opportunity and let his dark humour shine through. "There's a badge for that!" he announced.

The group erupted into laughter.

"Shhh!" Piper hissed. "My grandma is sleeping!" Her tone didn't match her face though, as she held a smile that Melody had never seen. An authentic Piper smile.

It wouldn't be that easy. Bringing Piper temporary happiness by dragging her ex-boyfriend to see her for a few hours would not keep her safe when they returned home. Melody now realized that she'd set Piper up for failure more than anything. They needed to convince Piper to go back to the hospital to keep her safe. They may have saved her tonight, but it wouldn't last forever.

"So, what now?" Piper said with a smile.

"I'm exhausted," Cody said. "That was a long drive, and it's almost my bedtime."

"You guys can come in; my grandma won't mind. I'll set us all up in the living room so we can get some sleep."

Everyone murmured in agreement. They followed Piper into the house and through to the living room, which closed with French doors. She turned the TV on and handed the remote to Tanner, before leaving to scrounge up some blankets and pillows. The guys spent the time arguing about what to watch, while Tanner flipped channels at lightning speed. There wasn't a lot to choose from that late at night, but ultimately a rerun of that week's Seinfeld episode won out. Melody and Piper sighed in teen-girl.

They each picked a spot on a couch or the floor and curled up without another word. Melody glanced up at the couch where Piper and Cody were spooning. *Why did they ever break up? This could have been a recreational road trip if they hadn't.* Melody's eyes drooped with fatigue, so she didn't give it another thought, and gave in to sleep.

CHAPTER 11
SEPTEMBER 1994
MELODY

Melody woke up first. She had always been an early riser, no matter what time she fell asleep. Jack, who had laid on the floor a few feet from her, had rolled so close that he'd thrown his arm over her in their sleep. She didn't dare move and took slow, shallow breaths, not wanting to wake him. Melody's intrusive thoughts stopped fighting for attention for the first time in weeks, mimicking the calm she experienced that day at the jumping rocks—like she was whole again.

As the sun rose outside the living room window, she watched it and smiled. This trip hadn't ended up like anything she'd been panicking about. It had actually turned out even better than she imagined. She needed to remember that the next time her logical mind checked out. Jack stirred beside her, so Melody pretended to sleep. She sensed him looking at her as he realized where his arm was, and he gently removed it and shuffled his body away from her on the carpet.

Melody wished she had a direct line to read his mind. Was he embarrassed or regretful, or like her, pleased with the accidental connection? Like most of Jack's feelings, those answers would remain a mystery, and she figured that was for the best—she couldn't be disappointed if she didn't know. At least she got to spend more time with him today, with both of them in a good headspace.

The rest of the group woke slowly, but they all received quite a fright when Piper's grandma came down the stairs, silent as a mouse, and then hollered at the top of her lungs after spotting four strange children in her living room.

"Oh, Grandma!" Piper said, gasping from the violent awakening, as she leapt up from the couch. "I'm sorry. I meant to tell you before you came downstairs. These are my friends from camp!"

Piper's grandma stared at them all, assessing the situation.

"Um, hi, good morning," she said, tightening her robe as she wandered off to the kitchen.

"Grandma, I'm so sorry I didn't catch you before you came down," Melody heard Piper whisper in the kitchen.

"Yes, that was quite a shock. I don't make a habit of young men seeing me in my nightgown!" Piper's grandma sounded annoyed, but she was still making jokes, so that was a good sign.

"My friends surprised me last night. They drove over three hours to come see me. Isn't that nice?" Piper continued.

"Nice, yes," her grandma mumbled as she cracked eggs into a pan. "They'll want breakfast then?"

"That's so kind, but you don't need to cook for them."

"Very well. You can cook for yourselves when I'm done in here. But make sure you clean up! And we need to have a discussion about this later. I'm not pleased you slept in a room with a bunch of boys last night."

"Yes, ma'am," Piper replied, and Melody heard her run upstairs, presumably to put herself together.

Melody shuffled into the kitchen as soon as Piper's grandma had left and searched for coffee. Piper returned, dressed and hair brushed, and she and Jack started prepping breakfast for everyone, as they were the most skilled in the kitchen. This gave

Cody, Tanner, and Melody a chance to sit out on the patio in the warm September morning and chat.

"I messed up. I'm sure I gave Piper the wrong impression last night by cuddling with her, but I was so relieved to find her alive, I couldn't help myself!" Cody said.

"I messed up too," Melody began. Cody and Tanner looked at her with surprise. "I brought everyone here and cheered her up for a few hours. But what is going to happen when we go home this afternoon? She'll be lonely and her mood might plummet, and she might be worse off than before we came."

Tanner sighed. "You both had good intentions. I wouldn't have come otherwise. Though I agree, we may have done more harm than good."

"So, now what?" Melody asked.

Tanner hesitated, biting his nails. "You need to tell her grandma."

"That will be a disaster," Cody replied.

"But she will get the help she needs," Tanner explained.

Melody stayed quiet. Piper opened the door and brought plates full of food out to them. She sat down next to Cody, and Jack brought out the rest of the meal.

The group chatted between bites and found out that Piper's mom had told her grandma that her brother wasn't getting any better and any hope of recovery had dwindled away—something the group felt too apprehensive to ask about the night before.

"They refuse to let me see him. They want me to remember him how he was. But I want to say goodbye." Piper's voice cracked, and she stopped talking.

Cody pulled her chair closer and wrapped his arms around her. Melody, trying not to cry herself, squeezed Piper's hand. No one knew what to say, so they said nothing. Piper returned to her breakfast, so the friends did too. The only sound around the table was the scraping of forks on their plates.

Melody, Jack, and Tanner tackled the clean up so that Cody

and Piper had some time to talk. Through the glass door, Cody looked like he might be sick. Melody wondered if the whole situation was more stressful for him than she had realized. The pair departed for a walk around the block for some privacy, but the trip didn't last long. A few quick minutes later, Piper threw open the front door and ran up the stairs, crying.

"What happened?" Melody asked Cody as he slumped into a kitchen chair.

"I tried to explain that she still needed to go get help, and that my coming here didn't mean we should be together. In hindsight, it may have been too much at once, but I didn't want to leave here sending mixed messages."

The friends sat around the living room, wondering what to do. Who should go upstairs and try to talk to Piper? Should they tell her grandma? What would be the next logical step? They decided Melody would attempt to smooth things over. She had been the one Piper reached out to, even though it was Cody's idea to come here, and Piper clearly didn't want to speak to him right now.

Melody crept up the stairs and listened at Piper's door before she knocked. Silence. Either she was no longer crying, or something more concerning was happening. Melody tapped on the door.

"Piper? It's Melody, can I come in?"

Piper didn't answer.

"Piper? I'm going to open the door, okay?"

Melody pushed the door open and found Piper sitting on the floor, staring into nothingness. She had her headphones on, which explained why she didn't answer, but she didn't flinch when the door opened, so maybe she had heard Melody after all. Either way, Piper looked like she wasn't really there. Melody sat down beside her.

"Are you okay?" she asked.

Piper didn't respond. Melody reached out and touched her hand to shake her from this zombie-like state. Piper flinched and snapped her head to look at Melody. She looked like she'd seen a ghost before she came back to reality.

"Melody? How long have you been there?" Piper asked, slipping her headphones off.

"Just a moment. You were in a daze," Melody answered. "What are you listening to?"

"If I Had a Boat. I miss camp so much."

Melody nodded. "Me too."

"Are the guys still downstairs?" Piper asked.

"Yeah, I wanted to come talk to you. We understand you're having a hard time, and we all want to help you…"

"But you think I'm too crazy to be friends right now?" Piper spit with her eyes narrowed.

"You're not crazy. My therapist said we shouldn't use that word, anyway. This is a lot. I've never dealt with anything like this before—"

"Your therapist?" Piper interrupted.

"Yeah, I started seeing one. It's already been helpful for me. That's why I think that if you checked back into the hospital for a bit and got yourself a little better, it would make an enormous difference for you."

"It's my fault. I shouldn't have gotten my grandma to check me out the first time. But I was drowning and everyone was just letting it happen. They weren't helping me get better," Piper explained.

Melody hesitated. "It's so hard to open up to people. Was it your mindset, maybe?"

Piper shrugged. "I was so fucked up when I got there. Actually, I'm still fucked up, but I have a better grip on reality this time. The thoughts haven't disappeared, so I might still try it again, but I know that it hurts others, and I don't want to do that to you guys and my grandma. I've screwed you all up enough."

Her nonchalance about suicide scared Melody. A few tears slipped down her cheeks, and she squeezed Piper's hand.

"Go for me, will you? Please? I want you to get healthy and for us to be friends. I want you to have the life you want," Melody whispered.

"Well, I'm not getting Cody back like this, so I guess I have nothing to lose," Piper said.

"So, you'll go?" Melody asked hesitantly.

"I'll go," Piper said as she hung her head in defeat.

Melody threw her arms around Piper and let out a massive sigh of relief.

"I'm so proud of you. You're going to do so well, and then we'll be able to hang out and celebrate the future instead of looking at the past."

"I hope that's true," Piper said.

CHAPTER 12
SEPTEMBER 1994
PIPER

Dear Diary,

How is it possible that I'm back here, and so soon? Grandma will never check me out of here against doctors' orders again. I cannot believe my friends came to my rescue and then sent me back here. I shouldn't even call them my friends. This betrayal is one for the ages. Cody doesn't want to be with me, Melody just wants to interfere in my life, Tanner is merely moral support for Cody, and Jack is, well, who knows, he doesn't seem to play any role in any of this. Though I think he loves Tanner and Melody loves him. What a tragic love triangle.

The worst part of being back here already is that I wanted to go visit Mitchell in the hospital. He's still in a coma, and Grandma says it sounds like he'll never wake up. I can't even process that news. I tried to get her to drive me home, to see Mama before she brought me here, but she said that would be a bad idea. Dad is out on bail for what he did to Mitchell, and there is surely a lot of tension between Mama and him. How could she even let him stay there after what he did? It's clear now I won't ever be going back to live with them, but I'm okay staying with Grandma. It's much calmer there.

I guess all I can do is try to get out of here as quickly as possible. I want to prove to Cody that I'm okay. That the girl he fell for is still here. And I need to see Mitchell. Plus, I want to go back to school so I don't lose my whole year again! I gotta get out of here, and fast, so if that means I have to play the perfect patient, that's what I'm going to be.

Piper spent her days following all the rules at Hoffman County Psychiatric Hospital. She took her meds without fighting, attended group therapy and actually contributed, took part in art therapy, and proved herself the model patient so they wouldn't just drug her up and leave her in her room to sleep all the time.

Piper called her grandma every day to check in, though her grandma eventually stopped answering the calls. It seemed like she was no longer interested in hearing about Piper's progress. Each day Piper remained locked away, she felt she was slipping further away from her life in the outside world.

After over three weeks in the hospital, Piper called her grandma again, expecting no answer, but this time, she answered the phone.

"Grandma? I'm almost ready to get out of here. Can you come pick me up on Sunday? The doctors will call you and speak to you before then."

"Piper, I'm sorry, with everything going on right now, I can't watch you 24/7. I already talked to your old caseworker, and she's going to find you a foster placement when you get discharged."

"What? I can't live with you anymore?" Piper cried.

"You haven't been here, Piper. Mitchell's doctors want to take him off the machines and let him go. Your dad is back in jail waiting for his trial. He already got in trouble again, so they revoked his bail. Your mama won't let go of Mitchell because right now he's all she has left. I have been trying to be who everyone needs, and it's too much. I'm almost 80!"

Piper dropped the phone and sank down to the floor. She knew for sure she wouldn't get to say goodbye to Mitchell now. She was stuck in a hospital, and so was he. The irony haunted her. She also didn't want to go back to foster care. Did Grandma have faith in their capability to keep her safe? Half the time, they don't even know the name of the kids in their house, let alone keep an eye out for them. Not to mention the awful houses and what happens in them. This could not be happening. *I thought if I came here to get better then everything would be okay when I got out.*

A nurse spotted Piper on the floor with the phone off the cradle, and rushed to her side. "What's wrong, Piper?"

"My grandma said I can't come home. She says when I get out of here, I have to go to foster care. They might take my brother off life support. My dad is in jail. My mama is all alone. I have to get out of here."

"Piper," the nurse began as she crouched to get eye-level with Piper, "this is even more reason to stay. You won't be safe out there yet. It sounds like there are a lot of hard things going on in your life right now. You will have the best support here."

"Until when?" Piper cried as she buried her head in her hands. "None of this stuff is going to get better or easier. I'm only going to prolong the inevitable if I stay here."

"That may be the case, but the longer you're here, the stronger and healthier you will be when you leave. You'll be more capable of dealing with all the hard stuff out there."

Not once did the nurse try to drag her off to bed for a medically-induced nap. *I guess working the program really does make a difference.*

Piper continued to call her grandma every day in the hopes she would change her mind. She needed her grandma to pick her up in time to say goodbye to Mitchell, and then take her home.

When she had been in the hospital for one month, her doctors gave her a progress update. Pleased with her cooperative behaviour this time, they assured her she was getting better, and that it seemed like they had figured out a good mix of medications to keep her bipolar disorder in check. This news surprised Piper. *Bipolar?* No one had ever told her that before.

The psychiatrist called Piper's grandma from the office line, so she wouldn't think it was Piper again, and put it on speakerphone so Piper could hear the conversation.

"Hi, Mrs. Shepard? It's Doctor Rigley. I'm calling about Piper."

"Yes?" Piper's grandma said expectantly.

"I have her here on speaker phone with me. As you know, Piper has been here for a month now, and she has made tremendous progress. We are very proud of her. She has worked very hard to heal and is getting stronger and healthier every day."

"Yes?" her grandma said again.

"Well, she is healthy enough to go home, however, we heard that there is a lot going on outside the hospital that may affect her mental health, and we wanted to check in with you," Dr. Rigley continued.

"Yes. I already explained to Piper that when she gets released, she will have to live in foster care."

Piper recoiled at her grandma's firm stance. Foster care hadn't seemed like too big a deal the first time she got out, because she was still in such a bad place, but now it would be so detrimental to her.

"And why is that?" Dr. Rigley asked.

"I can't handle her right now. She needs constant supervision, and I am already dealing with a lot."

"What if we kept her here for another two weeks? Would that make it easier on you? She would be even stronger when she got out. She wouldn't need supervision."

"No. I'm in the middle of dealing with the trial of my son and trying to convince my daughter-in-law that it's time to unplug Piper's brother from his life support. He's been on it for over almost two months now. Piper's mother will be a wreck when she makes that decision. I suspect she'll go down another destructive path that there's no returning from. None of that is going to get easier in the next two weeks."

"I see. Well, perhaps we will keep her here for another two weeks, and check in with you again. We're very sorry for everything you're dealing with," Dr. Rigley said.

"Okay, bye," her grandma replied, and hung up the phone.

Piper was a statue, frozen in disbelief. *Another two weeks in this place might kill me. I have been busting my butt every single day to get out of here at the one month mark, and now I have another two weeks. All because Grandma assumed I need a babysitter and won't let me come home. Not to mention, Mitchell will probably be gone whenever I get out of this place.*

Piper left the room without another word and shuffled down the hall to the common area. She figured it was a better strategy than burying herself in her bed. Instead, she zoned out on the couch to an episode of Boy Meets World. No one came to sit with her. Despite trying this time around, she had made no friends. She thought about Nicki and wondered how she was doing out in the world. *She isn't back here, so she must be okay.* Piper took comfort in that and settled in for the next two weeks of life.

She would make it out of there if it killed her.

The hours blurred into days, and eventually, it was time to call Piper's grandma again. They tried at nine o'clock, but she didn't answer. In fact, she hadn't answered all the days Piper had called to check in. She hoped nothing had happened since they last spoke. They tried again at noon, but they didn't have any luck. At three o'clock, when she still didn't answer, Piper panicked. She asked to call her mom, whom she hadn't spoken with since before she left for camp.

The phone rang half a dozen times before a sullen voice answered.

"Hello?" the woman said.

"Hello, Mama?" Piper asked, her voice wavering with nerves.

"Piper? Is that you?" the voice said.

"Yes, it's me."

"Oh, Piper, I've been so worried!" Her mom's voice, now recognizable. "Where have you been? You haven't called. Your grandma said you were getting some sort of treatment, but I had no idea where you were. You've been gone like three months!"

"I'm sorry. Since Grandma called with the news about Mitchell, I've been afraid to call the house. I didn't want Dad to answer. Mama, how is Mitchell?"

"Oh, baby, your grandma didn't tell you? My sweet Mitchell is gone. We took him off life support a week ago." Her voice trembled with heartache.

Piper sank to the floor and wailed. The grief crashed down on her, instant and debilitating. Her breath caught in her throat. Mitchell, her baby brother, her only sibling, was gone forever. Piper's mom cried now too. Suddenly, Piper remembered why Mitchell was dead.

"Mama. Where is Dad? Tell me he's locked away for the rest of his life."

"He's still in jail waiting for his trial. I've been alone at the house trying to keep rent paid, but it hasn't been easy. There's no money coming in with him gone. Are you coming home, baby? I sure could use a hand," Piper's mom turned on the charm like she always did.

Piper looked at Dr. Rigley, and at the nurse, and they both shook their heads.

"No, Mama. I am not coming home. I'm sorry you're struggling, but I'm struggling too, and we would make a mess of each other. Coming home isn't an option," Piper said with the utmost confidence, and Dr. Rigley beamed with pride.

Piper had figured it out this time. She was really getting better.

Her mom let out an audible cry. "Piper, I need you!" she wailed into the receiver.

Piper continued, "Mama, I'm sorry. I have to go. I'm sorry about Mitchell, and I will miss him for the rest of my life," Piper hung up as a little whimper escaped her lips and her throat constricted with the finality of the words. She slumped over in her chair.

After three days of crying, someone finally arranged a foster care placement for Piper. Despite battling the grief of losing her brother, and not even getting to say goodbye, Piper's mindset was strong. She no longer fantasized about ending her life. After losing Mitchell, she understood that death wasn't something that would "fix" anything. She wanted to live, she wanted to grow up and have a family of her own. One that was nothing like the one she was born into.

Piper had done the therapy and taken the medications, and she became healthier. She would have to continue working hard to stay that way, but she finally had the confidence in herself to do that outside in the real world.

CHAPTER 13

OCTOBER 1994
PIPER

They released Piper from the hospital into the care of Mark and Lisa Cotton the last week of October. Meeting foster parents had always been one of her least favourite things, but with a new plan for her life, she tried to make the best of it.

"Hi Piper," they crooned as the staff watched. Mark stood quite tall and looked a little rough around the edges, but dressed in a suit like he came straight from the office. Lisa had on a short dress with her blonde hair pulled back in a low ponytail, and had about a pound of makeup on her face.

"Hi," Piper said.

"We're so glad to meet you, Piper! Let's go home. You've got a pretty room waiting for you," Lisa said.

"Okay, thanks," Piper replied, avoiding eye contact, and exited the psychiatric ward doors. She gave one glance over her shoulder to Dr. Rigley, and he nodded. *Okay. I've got this.*

Leaving the hospital for the second time in as many months, Piper couldn't help but notice the change in the world around her. The daylight was still blinding, but the air smelled crisp, as each step she took crunched decaying autumn leaves in the parking lot. She'd never heard something so beautiful.

The golden leaves on the trees shone in the sun, and Piper's heart overflowed with joy as the breeze flowed through the open window. Fresh air always helped with her nerves. The drive was shorter than she would have liked, however. The last turn took them into a quiet middle-class neighbourhood, and Piper hoped she might end up somewhere decent for once.

The room at the Cotton's looked lovely, like they cared, or wanted it to appear like they cared, about their foster kids. There were three other kids in the house, all boys. One, the Cotton's biological son, and the other two were fosters. When Piper had a chance, she snuck off to where the two foster kids were hanging out in the backyard and asked them how it was living there.

"It's alright," the older one answered.

"As long as you follow the rules," the younger one added.

Piper didn't plan on breaking any rules, so she assured herself it would be fine. Besides, the bedroom beckoned for her after being in the hospital for so long. *Finally, freedom.*

After having time to settle in, the Cottons came up to Piper's room to explain the rules. They started out harmlessly enough:

1. No food in your room
2. No boys in your room
3. You must stay sober at all times
4. You must go to school every day
5. You must ask to leave the house
6. You cannot have a computer or TV
7. You cannot have friends over
8. You can only make pre-approved calls on the phone
9. You cannot go into the boys' rooms
10. You cannot take food without permission
11. You cannot contact your family without permission
12. You cannot tell anyone where you live

But they got a little more intense as the list continued, and Piper realized her earlier plans for freedom were a little premature.

"You might think our rules are very strict, but they ensure everyone stays safe, and the home is a happy environment," Lisa explained.

Yikes. Now it sounded more like prison. She might as well go back to the hospital. At least there she had a TV and the ability to make phone calls. It was clear to Piper from day one that she would never last in this house. She left her things packed in the backpack she took to the hospital, not even bothering to put her clothes in the dresser drawers. Those were all the possessions she owned now, though it was better that way. She'd be able to make a run for it anytime.

Piper started school the next day. The Cottons lived on a different side of town from her parents and grandma, so she had to attend a new school, but at least it gave her a fresh start where no one labelled her "the crazy one". She was grateful to have a second chance, though her stomach was still in knots about being at the Cotton's. They had opened her door to check on her every few hours through the night, which completely invaded her privacy, and was a little creepy.

Piper made it through the school day without a hitch, though she didn't make any friends, either. Starting over a month late meant that everyone had already developed their cliques. She figured it would take some time to find her people, so she didn't worry about it too much.

Piper made it home without getting lost, a pretty tremendous accomplishment for her. Lisa waited by the front door with a big smile plastered on her face. *Do people actually smile like that?* No one in her life ever had.

"Piper, dear, how was your first day?" she oozed.

"Fine, thanks. I have homework to do," Piper mumbled as she passed her and headed up the stairs.

"Would you like a snack?" Lisa called after her.

Piper was too unsettled to have an appetite, but with the "no food without permission" rule, she didn't know when she'd eat next, so she figured she should say yes.

"Yes, please, I'm starved," she said, dripping with fake enthusiasm.

Lisa disappeared to the kitchen to fix her something, and Piper shut her bedroom door to get started on her homework. Her missed weeks had left her behind her classmates, but her teachers had told her they understood her situation, not to worry too much, and to just do her best. Piper wasn't sure what exactly they'd been told, but it didn't sit well, regardless.

The boys had been right. The Cotton's house wasn't bad if you followed the rules—not always a simple task. A few days into her stay, she mentioned needing to go to the library after school to do homework, and Lisa had a fit.

"You cannot go to the library. You must come straight home. It's not safe for you out there. You need to be supervised."

"So, I'm going to be watched 24/7 while I'm here? I need to work on my research paper, and I don't have access to the proper books here."

"I will take you tonight to check out some books on your research topic," Lisa replied.

Piper groaned but said nothing in return. It was futile. They'd been arguing over the rules since she arrived. However, she knew she couldn't afford lower grades because of her inability to work at the library. *If I talk to my teachers, maybe they can do something about it.* Unfortunately, that was the first in a string of terrible decisions.

CHAPTER 14
OCTOBER 1994
PIPER

Bad decision number one: Piper told her new English teacher about how her foster home was affecting her ability to do her homework. She singled out the English teacher because she seemed like the warmest and most caring of the bunch. Unfortunately, the teacher misunderstood Piper's complaint of constant supervision as an indicator of a bigger problem, and called her foster parents to check in, not realizing that was a huge red flag.

Bad decision number two: Piper tried to cover up why the teacher had called with a lie, and then another, and a third. She wasn't familiar enough with Mark and Lisa to know whether they sensed she was lying, so she kept digging a bigger hole. She wanted to be sure they understood she didn't rat them out for anything, since they technically had done nothing wrong.

Bad decision number three: When her foster parents confronted her about the lying, she lied some more, and now Piper expected huge trouble when they figured it out. What kind of trouble remained unclear, however, it would come some way, somehow.

Bad decision number four: Because Piper now lied constantly, she was always in fear of getting caught, which caused her tenuous grip on her mental health to loosen. Her anxiety increased, something she rarely battled. Now at the mercy of her crappy government insurance, Piper wasn't sure how to go about getting a reputable therapist. She knew that the ones that were provided through the foster system were not that great and always had the placement parents in mind. Because she couldn't make unsupervised phone calls, she didn't reach out to anyone for help, despite the decline in her mental health affecting her daily.

Bad decision number five: Piper decided to run away. It was too much. The Cottons now watched her constantly at home, even making her sleep with her bedroom door open, and she felt her English teacher watching her at school too. The pressure was crippling.

Piper's thoughts became more paranoid each day, and she began having panic attacks at night while trying to fall asleep. She suspected this scenario would get worse by the day, and she wanted out before her head felt any worse. So, after only a few weeks at the Cotton's, Piper grabbed her always-packed backpack while everyone was in the kitchen making dinner, and she crept down the stairs and out the door.

From this point on, Piper found herself in a permanent fight-or-flight mode. She couldn't tell who to trust, if anyone at all. It had been so long since she'd talked to anyone from Sweet Clover that she didn't think they would even care where she was. But then again, they couldn't contact her because they didn't have her information.

Unfortunately, between her four quick moves; to the hospital, to Grandma's, back to the hospital, and then to foster care, her notebook with everyone's addresses and phone numbers had disappeared. A lifeline, lost and unable to help her.

Piper was on her own. The only person she might count on was her grandma. *Maybe she will take me in? At least for one night while I figure things out.* The house was on the other side of town, so Piper had a long walk ahead of her. Luckily, she had put fresh AA batteries in her hand-me-down Walkman before school that day, so her music kept her company.

The sun had set and Piper still had about an hour's walk ahead of her. Now chilled and tired, she wondered if she'd made a mistake.

Spoiler alert: she did.

While Grandma's house, in theory, seemed like a beacon of light and warmth, Piper pondered what she would find when she got there. Grandma had lost her son to prison after all, at least Piper assumed that's where he would be by now, and she'd buried her grandson, who had always been her favourite grandchild, anyway. But Grandma was the only hope Piper had, so she trudged along.

When she finally arrived at her grandma's, it was well into the "it's sketchy to knock on people's doors this late" time of the evening. Piper breathed a sigh of relief when she saw the living room light on though, as it meant her grandma must be home. She was so frugal she would never leave a light on if she had left the house. Piper knocked on the door and stepped back and to the centre, to allow her grandma to see her through the peephole, but no one came.

She listened for the sound of footsteps on the stairs. Nothing. She stepped back a little further and craned her neck to see the upstairs windows. She was sure she glimpsed a curtain moving, though it was hard to tell in the dark. Why wouldn't her grandma come to the door? It's not like Piper was a serial killer!

She pressed herself against the door and called softly, "Grandma? Grandma, it's Piper!", but she heard no response. Piper knocked a few more times.

Eventually she gave up, but it wasn't safe to continue wandering the city in the dark, so she crept around to the back patio. She peeked in the back door, but in the time that it took her to get around the side of the house, someone had turned the living room light off, and the house looked empty. Piper pulled all the cushions off the chairs and made herself a little bed with a roof to keep her comfortable and dry. It wouldn't keep her warm, but she would do her best to put on a bunch of the clothes in her backpack and hopefully not get frostbite overnight.

Thankfully, the little survival training she learned at camp kicked in, and a bit of her hard-to-find confidence shone through. She first pulled out the sandwich she'd saved from her lunch and enjoyed her meagre dinner with a few sips of water so she wouldn't run out. She had no plan for the next day, but for now, she needed to get through the night.

Piper started to pull each piece of clothing out of her bag. She had long-johns that she'd worn the one time in her life she went skiing on a school-funded trip. Her eyes darted around the yard one more time, and then stripped down to her underwear and put them on. Next, she put on knee socks pulled up over the legs. Then a pair of fleece track pants her brother had given her for Christmas the year before. He'd saved up every penny from his paper route to buy her something nice, and while she hadn't appreciated the choice then, they were saving her now.

"Thank you, Mitchell," she whispered into the dark night.

She dug through her bag for the next items she needed; a long sleeve t-shirt, and the forest green Camp Sweet Clover hoodie she'd bought that summer, before everything went to shit, with the money she'd made babysitting in her neighbourhood. Piper was sweating by the time she got her shoes back on and added a toque and stretchy mitts. They were the only winter gear she'd found in the closet at the Cotton's that afternoon. Overheating would pose a problem too, so she got into her cushion hut and laid still to allow herself to acclimate to the temperature and prevent excessive sweating. It did the trick, and she noticed a comfortable coziness within a few minutes.

Piper put her headphones over her toque and pressed play on

her Walkman again. The cassette tape turned, and Gin Blossoms came to life in her ears. Then she rolled over onto her side, pulled the notebook and pen from her backpack, and started writing. A habit was a habit, regardless of where she slept that night.

Piper hoped for a few hours of sleep and enough time to put the patio back together before her grandma woke. Relying on the sun and the birds to wake her in time, she crossed her fingers and closed her eyes. After her marathon of a walk, Piper had no trouble falling asleep, and when she awoke the sky was a dusty pink.

"Yes!" she whispered to herself and pumped her fist.

She peeked through a crack between the cushions and looked for movement through the patio door. Piper didn't see any, so with as much speed as her exhausted legs allowed, she put all the cushions back, shoved her water bottle and Walkman in her backpack and crept back around the house. Piper sat tucked between the garage door and the front bumper of her grandma's Buick, out of sight from the house and the street, while she came up with her next move.

It would make sense to knock on the door again before she left, though she needed to wait until her grandma woke up so as not to startle her. She was old, after all. The last thing she needed was a heart attack! Piper stayed camped out there until the street became busy with people leaving for work, and school buses started passing by. It must have been about eight o'clock, likely a safe time to knock on the door. She walked to the front of the house and knocked. After a minute had passed, she knocked again. And after the third time, her grandma threw open the door.

"Piper, what is with all this incessant knocking? If I'd wanted to see you, I would have called," her grandma said, sounding angrier than Piper had ever heard her.

"Grandma, I'm sorry, but I have nowhere to go. I need you."

Her grandma scoffed at this statement. "The hospital told me they set you up with a nice foster family. All you do is remind me of everything I've lost. I can't have you here."

Piper's heart sank, and she fought back tears. *This doesn't sound like my grandma. Is this what grief does?*

"I'm sorry, but the foster home was bad. I had to leave. Now I have nowhere to go."

Grandma looked Piper up and down and said, "why do you have so much clothing on? Where did you sleep last night?"

"On the street," Piper said. She didn't want her grandma to find out she'd been in the backyard the whole time.

"My word!" her grandma exclaimed, seeming to understand the gravity of the situation at last.

"Can I stay here, just for a little while, please?" Piper begged.

"I'm sorry, Piper. No. I can't have you here. You can come in for breakfast and a shower and then I will drive you back to your caseworker's office and you can get placed with another foster family. I can't be your parent right now."

Her grandma let her in and told her to sit while she made breakfast, but when Piper entered the kitchen, she realized why her grandma hadn't come to the door the night before. There were wine bottles all over the kitchen counter, and the house was trashed. It seemed like her grandma was doing as poorly as she let on, and Piper wrung her hands with guilt.

"Oh, Grandma, look at this place. Let me help you clean up, okay? After we can cook together like old times?"

"I can take care of my own house. Thank you very much!"

Piper stared at her for a moment, and with a quick nod, they got to work.

It didn't take the pair long to clean up the mess. Most of it was recycling anyway, followed by loading the dishwasher, and then wiping everything down. Piper wondered what the rest of the house looked like and whether she should help with that too. Her grandma seemed to be in an awful place mentally, and she was definitely drinking too much. It ran in the family, so it wasn't surprising.

"I'm going to wash up," her grandma said and sauntered up the stairs.

Piper took this opportunity to snoop around. Now might be her only chance. She dug through closets to find more of the clothing she'd left before the hospital, and made some PB&J sandwiches because she wasn't about to trust any of the meat or cheese in the refrigerator. A shower wasn't the priority right now.

When her grandma returned downstairs, her eyes grew wide as she saw Piper with a stack of four sandwiches, looking through the drawers for sandwich bags, but she said nothing and pulled the correct drawer out for Piper.

"Thank you."

"You can't stay here."

"Grandma, why? You need some company, and some help if I'm being honest. We'd be able to help each other."

"I am not fit to care for you right now. I am mourning my son, mourning my grandson. This is not the woman you once loved," she said, gesturing to herself with a vacant look in her eyes.

"Grandma, I am mourning too. But you're sending me away to do it in a foster home with strangers, where they don't treat me right, where I can't get the therapy I need. I want to be with you."

"I'm sorry for what I said earlier, but you need better. Go on, get in the car," her grandma said.

Piper didn't argue. There was no point. The discussion was over. It would be better to leave on good terms. That way, her grandma might come around at some point. She drove Piper to the Child Protective Services building without another word.

Ugh. Another placement. What will they say about me running away? That will be on my record now, and it might cause families to turn me away.

It occurred to Piper the way she was reacting to all of this, or not reacting to it, rather, was unlike her. For the first time, she recognized that being in the hospital had made her healthier and stronger. She wasn't angry, she wasn't panicked, she was just taking things as they came. She would take her new placement as it came too, and hope for the best. *This family might be lovely. Maybe it will be a positive experience until Grandma is ready to have me home. I could like it there, if I try, right?* Of course, all these decisions were far too hopeful, far too soon.

CHAPTER 15
OCTOBER 1994
PIPER

Piper spent her entire day in a tiny office, waiting for her new foster family to pick her up. She wondered if it would be the fresh start she was hoping for. *Will I have to start at another school for the third time this year? That would be unbearable. Will I have better rules?* Piper also couldn't let go of her last interaction with her grandma. She had dropped Piper at the door, said goodbye, and drove off. Her grandma had always been a sort of frigid woman, however, this experience took it to another level. Piper assumed the guilt had gotten to her, and she simply hadn't wanted to show her emotions.

Steven and Maggie Brussels arrived at six o'clock, after Piper had been alone and bored all day long. She thanked earlier-Piper for packing those sandwiches, because while the CPS staff offered her some lunch, it was obviously something leftover they had lying around. Piper took one look at the couple and could already tell that the placement would be a bad time. It was quite apparent, to her at least, that they had dressed the part to come and pick her up. They were not as clean cut as they were projecting. She had enough experience in her short life to identify a scammer when she saw one, or in this case, two.

"Hello Piper, we've heard so much about you," Steven drawled.

"Um, hi," Piper said before looking at her caseworker to signal for help with only her eyes.

"We're so excited to bring you home. We've got your room all set up! It's only you right now so you don't even have to share, isn't that great?" Maggie crooned.

"Uh, yeah, great," Piper replied.

Being the only kid sounds like winning the lottery, until something bad happens and you have no one to back you up or help you through it.

The house was dark when they pulled in. Piper had tried to follow all the turns they made to help her navigate her way back out if needed, but sometime around the fourth turn in the middle of a subdivision, in the dark, she got confused. Steven and Maggie hopped out of the car and looked in the window at Piper.

"Well, come on," Steven said.

Piper followed the couple into the house. The street had seemed decent and well-kept, though inside the house was a different story. She could imagine that once upon a time the house looked nice, but now it appeared dated, dirty, and void of any personality. It wasn't the warm, sophisticated illusion they portrayed for her caseworker. Piper feared what her room may look like. *Could it get worse than this?*

"Your room is up the stairs to the right. We'll let you settle in and get some dinner ready," Maggie said.

Piper climbed the stairs as if they were mounting to her doom. Her heart raced and her hands got clammy for the first time that day. It was so quiet. A byproduct of being in a home with no other kids. She hadn't ever experienced that in any of the placements she'd been in.

Piper opened the door and her eyes grew wider by the second. Inside, she found a pretty, dusty-pink room, with a modern metal bunk bed covered by a mint comforter on each mattress. A white desk with a work lamp and a clock stood on the other side of the room. There were white curtains on the window and a closet with mirrored doors to the right. This looked like a perfect preteen girl's room in the suburbs.

So, what was the catch? Why would the rest of the house be in such disrepair and this room so nice and brand new? She put her bag in the closet and laid down on the bottom bunk. After sleeping outside the night before, the bedroom felt like a dream come true, and she became cautiously optimistic that she would get an amazing night's sleep.

"Piper, dinner is ready," Maggie called up the stairs.

After eating nothing but two PB&J sandwiches that day, because she and Grandma hadn't even gotten to making breakfast after they cleaned up that morning, Piper was ready for a meal. It did not surprise her to find pasta on the table waiting for her, as it was a staple in foster homes. Cheap, fast, and most of the kids could make it themselves by the time they were six or seven.

"Smells good, thanks," Piper said, trying to put her best foot forward.

Maggie smiled, and they all dug in. After Piper satiated her hunger, she tried to figure out her situation a little better. She had to be cautious about what she asked, but she needed to get as much information as possible.

"So, will I be starting school tomorrow? What school is it?"

Steven replied, "Yes, I'll drive you on my way to work. It's Cavanaugh Secondary."

"Oh man, another school. That's the third one this year," Piper groaned.

"Well, if you hadn't run away from your last home, that wouldn't be an issue, would it?" Maggie snipped.

"Sorry Piper, that's not about you. We had a kid run away a few weeks ago. It's hard on the parents. It still hurts Maggie," Steven explained.

Piper was unsure how to respond, so she took a sip of her water instead.

"Do you have questions?" Steven prompted her.

"Um, do you always have only one kid? I've never been in a home without a handful of kids running around."

"Yes, we like to focus on one child at a time so we can help them grow and thrive," Maggie said.

The answer sounded very scripted. *If they were focusing on helping a child grow and thrive, why did a child run away from their home?*

"Well, the bedroom is lovely." Piper started, "The nicest I've ever had."

"Thank you," said Maggie. "It's an older house and we're aware it looks kind of dated. We just moved in a few months ago, and we are trying to fix it up one room at a time, so the bedrooms were first."

Piper struggled to wrap her head around this interaction. Steven and Maggie seemed nice enough, and her room was beautiful, but she couldn't shake the instinctual mistrust that their first impression gave her. Wolves in sheep's clothing. She wondered if her gut no longer functioned correctly. After all, her brain was in check after being properly medicated and she felt healthier than she had in a long time. Maybe her gut had always been a by-product of her mental illness. Perhaps this time she needed to listen to her heart instead.

"Will you work on the main floor next?" she asked, to feign interest in their lives.

"Yes, Maggie has it all planned out. Hopefully, you can help us with some of it this weekend. We'd love to spend more time getting to know you," Steven said through a too-wide grin.

"Sure. I'm pretty tired though, I'm going to head up to bed."

"Okay, honey," Maggie gushed, her mood flipped.

Piper took the flight of stairs up for the second time, now with her optimism restored, and looking forward to an incredible night's sleep. But as always, her hope was premature and that incredible night's sleep didn't come.

Piper had just drifted off when she heard her door creak open.

She looked over at the desk to check the time—one o'clock. She squeezed her eyes shut and pretended to be asleep. Her heart raced and her breath was louder than she could hope to hide.

Steven tiptoed over to Piper's bed and carefully dragged the covers down. Piper faked waking up, about to scream her refusal, but he was quicker and clamped his hand down hard on her mouth. Her gaze changed from panic to sheer terror, as she comprehended what was coming next. This wasn't the first time it had happened, but she prayed it would be the last. No amount of squirming would allow her to overpower Steven's six-foot-three body, so she didn't even try. She would need that energy later to run.

When Piper felt her consciousness return to the room, Steven was gone, and the sky was still dark. She pulled her track pants back up her legs and worked quickly to gather her things. Thankfully, her struggling brain had one redeeming feature— blacking out during traumatic events. Piper often only figured out what happened in those scenarios from the physical clues left behind. *I can't believe I gave up the Cotton's for this.*

Not daring to risk waking Maggie or Steven on her way to the front door, Piper opened her window, climbed onto the small, peaked roof, and jumped into the grass. Her battered lower-body screamed with the impact, but her adrenaline kicked in to help her overcome her pain, and she took off down the street as fast as her legs would carry her. Piper decided she would never step foot in another foster home as long as she lived.

CHAPTER 16
OCTOBER 1994
PIPER

The Rose Project, a local shelter for women and children, awaited Piper just down the street. She had stayed there with her mom once before, when her dad stopped paying the rent and they became homeless. It was a devastating time for her as a child, but the muscle memory of which streets to take to get there was saving her life.

She arrived in the parking lot shortly before dawn. It had taken a long time to get across the downtown through physical discomfort and unbearable mental anguish. Opening the door, she collapsed to the floor, exhausted and done, like she had felt that day at camp. Piper laid on the tile and sobbed, not even able to bring herself to stand.

The staff member at the front desk rushed to her, asking what help she needed, as she gently raised Piper to a seated position. Piper leaned on the woman and continued to cry. Eventually, the woman stretched out to reach the tissue box on the desk and handed a few to Piper.

"Thank you," she said through sniffles.

"My name is Mable, honey. You hurt? Did something happen that we should deal with right now? Or do you just need a bed?"

Piper didn't know.

"Do you want to take a hot shower?"

Piper nodded. She was frozen from the walk in clothing that wasn't exactly appropriate for late October nights. Mable showed her to an empty bed in a room with eight bunks. All but one were full of sleeping women.

"Put your things down and I will get you a clean towel," Mable whispered.

Piper followed her out of the room and down the hall. They stopped at a large closet and she handed Piper a bar of soap and a bath towel, and ushered her further down the hall towards the bathroom.

"Here you go. If you need anything, I'll be at the front desk. Breakfast is at seven o'clock."

"Thank you," Piper whispered before shutting the door and locking it.

Piper watched the scalding water cascade down her body and couldn't help reliving the sensation of Steven climbing on top of her mere hours before. She wondered what would come next. Despite the crippling sorrow and disgust she grappled with, going to the police wouldn't do her any good. They would take a statement and promise to "investigate", and throw her right into another foster home. She stayed in the shower far too long, trying to shove the flashbacks out of her head and calm herself before getting out, but eventually there was a knock at the door. Piper froze.

"Excuse me, are you almost done? I need to get in there," a woman's voice said.

"Sorry, I'm getting out!" Piper called through the door.

Piper padded back to the room with bare feet, her arms full of her clothes. She sat on her bed, still in her towel, and searched her bag for cozy clothes to put on. She checked the clock; it was almost time for breakfast. Piper wandered out of the room with a vague memory of meals being served near the end of the hall, and then followed the sounds of chatter to a large gymnasium.

There were so many women, and a handful of children too. The room was loud and chaotic, but also warm, and it smelled like pancakes. Piper noticed that she somehow felt a semblance of calm amidst it all, and walked around the room until she found an empty table. She sat down and watched, trying to sort out the logistics.

Mable entered the gym and encouraged people to get in line. She found Piper on her own and waved her over. Piper stood and walked to meet Mable.

"Have a good shower?"

"Yes, thank you," Piper replied.

"Wonderful. You can line up here for breakfast. Everybody gets the same amount, and if there are leftovers, people can come up for seconds, okay?"

Piper nodded.

"Will you meet with the director when she comes in at nine o'clock? She can tell you more about our programs here and get you set up with whatever social services you need, okay?"

Piper nodded again.

"Great! Enjoy your breakfast!" Mable called as she walked back towards her station at the front desk.

Piper wasn't hungry, but as usual, where her next meal would come from was unclear, so she needed to get some food in her. She watched the other women in the room, and most looked as weary as she did. When she couldn't stomach anymore food, Piper grabbed a cup of coffee and returned to her bed. She didn't have many belongings now, so she was nervous about leaving them alone for too long. She sat on her bed and enjoyed her coffee while she waited for her appointment time.

A few minutes before nine, Piper traipsed back to the front of the building, seeing it in a little more detail this time, and asked Mable where she should go. Mable pointed her in the office's direction. Piper knocked on the door, and a woman on the other side invited her in.

"Hi, I'm Victoria."

"I'm Piper," she said without looking up from the floor.

"Hi, Piper. I heard you came in early this morning. Have you settled in?"

"Yes, I took a shower and had some breakfast."

"Wonderful," Victoria began, "and may I ask, how old are you, Piper?"

"I'm sixteen," Piper answered.

"Okay, and how did you end up here at The Rose Project?"

"I ran away from my foster home. They were… not the best people," Piper answered, not wanting to divulge too much information.

"Did they hurt you?" Victoria asked.

Piper nodded.

"Would you like to see a doctor?"

Piper fought against every impulse to say no and run from there, but she opened her mouth and what fell out was a "yes". She needed an exam, and a prescription for the medications to prevent infections and a pregnancy. Why did it always feel like she was fighting multiple parts of herself just to survive?

"Okay, we have a doctor that makes house calls so you don't even have to leave the facility. I will have her come by to see you today," Victoria explained, "and because you're sixteen, you can stay here; however, we will need to check in with your CPS caseworker and share what's happened, is that okay?"

Piper wasn't sure, so she didn't answer.

"How about we revisit that later, after you've seen the doctor?"

Piper nodded again.

"I need you to fill out some information for me. It's for our system only. We don't share this with anyone without your permission. Is that okay?"

Piper finally got up the courage to speak. "Yes."

"Most of the children here have already gone off to school, and many of the women will leave for work soon. So, for now, why don't you rest, catch up on some sleep, and take some time for yourself? I will notify you when the doctor is coming."

"Thank you," she whispered.

Victoria slid the paperwork over to Piper and left the room. Piper was relieved that it requested only the basics like her name, birthday, and last school she attended. Piper did her best to fill out what she could, then doodled on the corners of the paper while she waited for Victoria to return.

"What's this?" Victoria asked, pointing to the corner of Piper's paper.

"Oh, sorry, I shouldn't have doodled on the form."

"No, it's fine. I only ask because I am curious," Victoria assured her.

"Um, I grew up going to this summer camp, and we earned badges. Kind of like Scouts, you know? I never earned very many, but my friends and I have a joke about getting badges for… extra-curricular activities that aren't always super healthy."

Victoria, avoiding the fact that she was starting at a badge with a pill on it, said, "It's nice you have camp friends and fond memories!"

Piper nodded.

"Go rest, Piper. I'll find you in time for your appointment," Victoria said.

Yes, please. Sleep will give me some relief from these intrusive thoughts. Piper gave Victoria an apprehensive smile and retreated out the door and back towards her bed.

CHAPTER 17

OCTOBER 1994
PIPER

The doctor came to see Piper that afternoon, and referred her to the therapist, who also made house calls to the shelter. The doctor suggested Piper speak with the therapist before they decided whether to contact CPS. Victoria agreed and had the therapist come in for an emergency session that evening.

The quickest way to get all this logistical nonsense over with would be to tell the therapist exactly what happened, despite Piper not even being able to comprehend it herself. The therapist, however, didn't even flinch. Obviously, this was something she heard often from the women here.

"Piper. You have been through a lot in the foster system, and it might trigger you if you return. I am going to recommend that Victoria make a call to the police to report the assault and let them handle it from there without you having to be involved. Victoria said you can keep the bed as long as you need it, but she expects you to work toward supporting yourself, as the other women here do. The facility is a stop-over, not a permanent home. Okay?"

Piper nodded.

"I'm also going to make sure you have a good supply of your

medications, so you don't need to worry about those running out."

"Oh, thank you," Piper said, relieved. That hadn't even crossed her mind until now, but it would be a nightmare if she were to run out of her medication. She didn't want to get back to that dark place mentally. Things were going to be tough enough living at the shelter. She didn't need her bipolar disorder, making it harder.

The therapist left, and Piper checked in with Victoria.

"I agree. I will make the report now, but you don't need to be involved."

"Thank you. I don't want it to happen to anyone else, but I don't think I can go on record, or even worse, have to testify in court," Piper explained.

"That's understandable. Thanks, Piper."

"Thank you. I really feel better already," Piper shared.

As Piper ventured down to dinner, she wondered what the other women here were like, and if they would they be nice to her? She didn't want to continue eating alone. Two meals were depressing enough. She got in line and heard someone come up behind her.

"Hi," a little voice squeaked.

Piper turned around and found another girl about her age standing there.

"Hi," Piper said back.

"I'm Emma. You're new?" the girl asked. She was blonde with curious blue eyes and had freckles splattered across her nose. She smiled at Piper.

"Yes, I got here this morning. My name is Piper."

"Welcome to the Rose. It's nice here. You'll like it. Are you going to go to school?" Emma asked.

"Yes, I start tomorrow. Will you show me where it is?" Piper asked.

"Definitely!"

Piper sought an empty table and sat down with her meal. Emma followed her and chose the seat across from her.

"So, how long have you been here?" Piper asked.

"A few weeks," Emma replied.

"How old are you?" Piper asked between mouthfuls of soup—finally hungry.

"Sixteen. You?" Emma said.

"Me too," Piper replied with a hint of a smile.

The girls chatted throughout dinner, and it relieved Piper to find out she wasn't the only teenager here on her own. She crawled into bed that night feeling safe for the first time since she left the hospital. It was strange to be in a room full of bunk beds and unfamiliar people and to still feel safe. *It's just like camp. A cabin full of strangers, all nestled in their bunks.* She hoped she would connect with some women over the next few days. But first she had to worry about school. Her third one in less than two months.

Piper tossed and turned all night and still woke up bright and early for school. Victoria had registered her the day before, so Piper was all set to go that second morning. She showered, much more quickly this time, and got ready for the day, and waited by the front desk. Emma was going to show her the ropes, and Piper's gratitude for already having a friend at school brightened her morning. She worried, though, about meeting anyone else. Life for a foster kid was hard enough. That came with a pretty disparaging stigma hanging over your head, and now she was homeless and living in a shelter. Surely kids would view that even more poorly than a foster home.

Piper figured it wouldn't be that tough to keep where she lived a secret but made a note to ask Emma how she approached it, because if Emma hadn't been discreet, then kids would already guess when they showed up together. She didn't want to start her first day undercover, but she didn't also couldn't handle the stares she would get if she told the truth about where she lived. Emma came to the front a few minutes later and put Piper's mind at ease.

"Hey, Emma? Have you told the kids at school where you live?"

"Oh, no!" Emma said through a laugh. "That is the last thing I want to share. It's not exactly common, or a pretty picture—a homeless sixteen-year-old living at a shelter. I don't need people pitying me or assuming I'm messed up or bad news because of where I live. The school is liberal, and the kids are pretty accepting, but that's not the type of information I would put on a button."

"Oh, good." Piper breathed a sigh of relief.

They spent the rest of the trip to school in silence, which was fine with Piper. The exhaustion had taken over, and she was neither chatty nor a morning person on a good day. It was different with her camp friends. Well, it had been. They arrived at school after a quick 10-minute bus ride, and Emma walked Piper to the office to pick up her schedule.

Snatching it out of Piper's hands, Emma said, "We have two classes together! That's so great! English first period, and Science fourth period."

"Rad!" Piper replied with a grin.

The coverage of her day's start and end prevented her from getting lost going to the bus stop, so she only needed to navigate two classes on her own. For years, minor victories were how she had stayed afloat amid the chaos, and this seemed like it qualified.

Piper had an uneventful day. The classes she had with Emma were almost fun, and the other two she kept to herself but didn't really feel nervous. The best part was that none of the teachers singled her out as the new girl or made her tell the class anything about herself. When she asked Emma if that was normal, Emma let Piper in on a little secret. The school had a high population of foster kids and kids in other uncertain circumstances, and consequently lots of students coming and going throughout the year. Everyone just sort of glossed over it all to be as unobtrusive as possible in these kids' lives.

Piper loved that. In all her other schools, it was always a big deal that she was new and starting part way through the year. Instead of being uncomfortable, this first day was one of the best she had ever experienced, and she might actually have a future at this school.

"No wonder my anxiety wasn't taking over. It's so great to be around kids like us for once!"

"What do you mean?" Emma asked.

"You know, broken. It's like we get each other."

Emma looked at the ground without responding.

"Did I say something wrong?" Piper asked.

"I don't like being called broken," Emma raised her voice.

Before Piper had time to apologize, Emma was climbing up the bus steps. Piper followed her on, but Emma sat next to someone else. Deflated, Piper picked a bench alone.

Victoria and the therapist had told Piper she was welcome to stay at the shelter as long as she progressed and could support herself, so doing well in school was step number one—including making friends. She hoped she'd hadn't blown it with Emma already. That was so typical of her to fuck something up before it even got good.

Next on her list, once she had settled in, would be to find a part-time job. She had never had a job before, but now that she would have some stability and a constant supply of her meds, she should be able to handle that. Piper also decided she should try to get a driver's license too, but considering she didn't currently have a home, it wasn't likely she'd have a car soon, and that goal could wait a little longer.

The last thing on her list was the biggest. Piper wanted to start fresh and reclaim all the years she'd lost. Every year she spent fighting to stay alive, every dramatic event that had caused her or others to hurt, every friendship she'd lost with her constant moving and losing touch. She was going to get it all back, and it started right now.

PART TWO
SAY IT AIN'T SO

CHAPTER 18
AUGUST 1995
MELODY

Melody sat at her desk, drumming her fingers, staring at a blank white page. She was attempting to write a letter to Jack, this time knowing it was going across the country. They had kept in touch over the last year, with phone calls every couple of months, and sending letters and CDs back and forth to each other's mailboxes.

Then, in July, Melody received a letter from him with a new address in Nova Scotia. Her mouth had fallen open in shock, not only by the cross-country move, but by the news of his long time girlfriend, someone he had never mentioned until now.

That was one of Jack's many talents—compartmentalizing people, places, and things in his life and pulling them out only when he wanted to. Usually, she loved that about him. When they spent time together, it was just the two of them. There were never any outside people or situations influencing their time together. Their friendship seemed to exist in a vacuum.

But now, this trait had become something else, almost like she wasn't important enough to hear these pieces of news in advance. It made it seem like things that were obviously important in his life sprang up out of thin air, and she felt betrayed by the suddenness of it all. Her heart ached with how little she knew about him; how little she must mean to him.

When Melody had opened that letter, instead of the excitement she usually felt bubble up in her chest by the surprise contact, she sat in her room and cried. While the news of her long distance best friend becoming an even longer distance best friend would not affect her day-to-day life all that much, finding out he was living across the country with someone he didn't even care to tell her about, made her wonder what else she didn't know, or if she was as close with him as she thought.

All these ideas were stewing in her soul, while she stared at the blank page, willing herself to write happy, supportive sentiments, all the while wanting to send him anything but.

August 1, 1995

Jack,

Wow, Nova Scotia! That's a big change! It must be pretty exciting to get a fresh start like that—new province, new school, new girlfriend. Well, I guess she's not new anymore?

I have had a really busy summer so far, but I wish we could have hung out and said goodbye before you left. How long had you been planning this move? It must have been sudden since you didn't call and let me know first.

I hope everything works out just the way you planned. Will you be coming home for the holidays? It would be nice to get together. Maybe I could meet your girlfriend?

Miss you, always.

Melody

It took Melody four days of writing and erasing and restarting to come up with a letter that sounded congratulatory enough, while also subtly conveying that he hurt her feelings. She never had to share anything like this with him before, and writing it down made her sick to her stomach. He was supposed to be the one who never hurt her, who always made her smile, who knew exactly when she needed a letter or a phone call. He was the sun.

CHAPTER 19
MARCH 1999
MELODY

Dear Diary,

It's been a while since I've written. Years, probably. It's funny how sometimes we neglect things that are so beneficial for us when we need them most. The only writing I've done, besides the never-ending pile of school assignments, is to Jack. I miss him so much, more than he misses me, I bet. We were corresponding every few weeks when we first got home from London, but I guess he got busy with his second year of university, and his girlfriend, after transferring to Nova Scotia. He never shared much about himself in the letters. He excels at tucking pieces of his life away. I know that it's just his personality, and I should get used to it.

As the letters came further and further apart, I eventually stopped writing to him unless he wrote me first. He reached out once or twice a year, but by that time I had gotten busy with my own social life, and trying to figure out what I was doing with my future. Eventually, my excuse became the busyness of graduating, parties, and summer jobs before starting university.

Rather than my childhood dream of being a journalist, I pursued psychology. Can you believe it? Because of everything I have gone through, with my anxiety and the trauma of saving Piper from committing suicide, twice, I realized I wanted to help people, like I helped Piper... I mean, I think I helped Piper. I wonder where she is now. It's strange that I felt so connected to her all those years ago, and then she just disappeared. I sent a few letters after we left London, but I never heard back from her. I hope she's okay.

If I'm being truly honest though, choosing psychology might have been because as a journalist you can get surface level information to share with the world, but as a therapist I could find out peoples' deepest darkest secrets instead and keep them close to my chest. Nosiness doesn't go away as you get older, apparently!

It's wild how far I've come from thinking therapy was only for "sick" or "crazy" people, to attending regularly, and studying to become a therapist myself. The only problem with this plan is that my social anxiety, which we haven't ever found a solution for, makes me not want to be a practicing psychologist. Those one-on-one appointments seem daunting, and I have yet to figure out a comfortable way to use my degree when I finish. But that's a problem for future-Melody. For now, I'm just doing the work.

I guess that's why I'm picking you back up. My

program talks a lot about how revolutionary journaling can be for your mental health and personal development. It is also bringing me back to my love of writing, so that's good for me too. I've wanted to write to Jack again recently. It's been too long, and though we aren't completely cut off from each other, letters just have a special something, don't they? Maybe this is my gateway back to that part of our relationship.

Melody

University was gruelling, and it took a lot out of Melody. She had no time to spend with friends and she barely left her desk unless it was for a trip to the library. Without social connections, her favourite pastime had become listening to camp songs while she worked. It always reminded her of the summers she spent in her favourite place and gave her hope that one day she would find her way back there.

Near the end of her second year of university, a knock at the door startled Melody. She walked down the stairs and peered out the front window. Her heart leapt into her throat and she flung the door open.

"Jack! What are you doing here?" she squealed.

He beamed his classic Jack smile and didn't even get a word out before she crashed herself into him for a hug. It had been two years since they'd seen each other in person, and he squeezed her so tight her ribs protested. He smelled like camp. Not the physical place, but the memories of her time there. When he let her go, there were tears in her eyes. If Jack noticed, he did her the favour of not mentioning it.

"How's it going, kid?" he teased.

"I can't believe you're here. What are you doing in Ontario?"

"I'm home."

"Like for good? You're moving back?" Melody asked, eyes wide.

"Yup. I finished college and tried to find a job and settle into adult life, but I just couldn't do it. I realized that Nova Scotia didn't have what I needed, so I came back for... well, we need to talk. Can I come in?"

Melody opened the door wider and gestured for him to enter. Words escaped her now. *He came back for what? For whom?* They sat on the couch in the front room and Melody tried to deep breathe through her heart trying to break its way through her chest wall. She looked at him impatiently, waiting for whatever news he planned to spring on her that would seem sudden despite it going on behind closed doors for who knows how long.

"I came back for Tanner," Jack blurted out.

The shock spread across Melody's face. "For Tanner," she repeated.

"For Tanner," Jack echoed.

"You're... gay?" Melody questioned as her gears turned and every bit of their relationship clicked into place in her mind.

Jack let out a huge laugh. "Oh gosh, no!" He paused. "Just bi!"

"Wow, bisexual, really? And you're in love with Tanner?"

"I am. I mean, I'm pretty sure I have been since like... 1994," Jack said through a sheepish smile, one Melody had never seen before.

"Well, I love that for you!" Melody pulled him in for another hug. "Tanner is the literal best, and if I have to lose you to someone, I'm glad that it's him!" She winked to make it clear she was being facetious.

"Lose me?" Jack raised an eyebrow with a grin. "You're not losing me Melody Burton, you're getting me back. I'm going to be less than two hours away now!"

"You're absolutely right."

"So, are you surprised?"

"Um, now that I'm processing this information, no, I'm not at all!"

"Well, you could have told me!" Jack jokingly elbowed her and all the tension seemed to melt from his body. He slumped back into the couch, and Melody joined him in a moment of comfortable silence.

Jack stayed for the entire afternoon. Out for a walk to enjoy the warmth that had finally returned, he divulged more to Melody than ever before, and she couldn't help but predict this as a turning point in their friendship, even if it was moving the opposite direction from what she had envisioned.

"I was always hiding parts of myself away. From everyone in my life. It was so stressful to keep all the pieces of me separate, but I also hadn't even figured out what all those pieces were yet. I should have tried to talk to someone about it, I guess. Figuring out that I love Tanner allowed me to open the boxes and let the emotions be as they were, chaotic and free, not separate and controlled. Does that make sense?"

Melody was out of her depth here. She knew all the right things to say, thanks to her schooling, but as a non-neutral party in this conversation, she struggled to find the words. Instead, she just nodded.

"Tanner and I kept things platonic while I lived in Nova Scotia, but once I figured things out, it quickly developed into something more, so I had to move home."

Melody wanted to ask about the girlfriend he had moved to Nova Scotia for, but decided it didn't matter anymore.

"And how are you doing? What's new? I haven't seen you in forever! Is there anyone special I should know about?" Jack asked as he stopped and looked Melody in the eyes while she answered.

"No, no one special. I've been focusing on surviving school. There's no time for anything else."

Not like I was waiting for someone else, or anything. Maybe I can open myself up a bit more to the possibility of a relationship with someone now.

Later that afternoon, Jack left her with a kiss on the cheek, a hug long enough to last through spring, and the promise of seeing each other that summer. Melody returned to her desk to continue studying, but her brain felt like mush with all the information she was processing.

CHAPTER 20
APRIL 1999
MELODY

Melody had one exam left to pass, in her toughest class, psychopathology. Predicting it might help to study with classmates for once; she called a few of her friends in the class and planned a Thursday night study session at the library. Everyone agreed quizzing each other on medication uses would be more helpful than reading them repeatedly. Melody suggested they each invite anyone who would be a helpful study partner, so Sarah showed up with Riley, Jessica showed up with Miles, Becky showed up with Megan, and Melody came alone.

She had never spoken to Riley, Miles, or Megan, though she was familiar with them from their lectures together. The group settled into one of the cozy study rooms in the library. It featured comfy chairs and a coffee table, with a few floor pillows for extra seats. Melody and Riley ended up on the floor beside each other and exchanged polite introductions while they unpacked their bags.

The group dove right into studying, as they knew they had a long night ahead of them. Their productivity didn't last long, however, because Riley seemed determined to chat with Melody instead of quizzing her. He interrupted her concentration multiple times, but inexplicably, Melody found it endearing instead of frustrating. Eventually, they returned to Melody's meticulous study cards, and instead of chatting, shared flirty looks over their textbooks.

At close to midnight, the group of seven agreed it was time for bed. Their exam was at eight o'clock, and they needed to be well-rested.

As Melody got up to leave, Riley said, "Can I walk you to your car? It's pretty late."

Melody hesitated; but she appreciated the offer and agreed to let him accompany her. They sauntered through the eerily empty campus to the west parking lot. Riley talked about his job at Starbucks, and Melody shared how isolating she'd found their second year to be with the intense workload, and how it was astonishing that he could hold down a job too.

"It's not an option for me to not work, unfortunately," Riley explained. "I have to pay my way through school, and I'd like to leave campus in two years without $100,000 worth of debt!"

"Well, that's pretty impressive that you're managing all of those things at once," Melody offered.

"Oh, sure, but I haven't had a home cooked meal or seen my friends since Christmas! The sacrifice will be worth it one day, but right now, it sucks!"

Relatable. Being far away from the place you called home and the people that felt like spring sunshine on your skin was a challenge she had faced too.

Walking in the quiet, Riley gently bumped into her side, and slid his hand into hers. Melody, surprised but flattered, looked up and gave him a small smile. He stopped walking and looked her in the eyes, as if looking for confirmation they were on the same page, before making his next move, then slowly pulled her around to face him. Melody's heart leapt into her throat and her palms got instantly damp with nervous sweat, but Riley didn't seem to mind.

Staring at their hands before peaking at Melody out of the corner of his eye, Riley asked, "Can I kiss you?"

A reply wasn't necessary. Melody made the decision without hesitation, maybe for the first time in her life, and stood up on her tiptoes to place her lips on Riley's. Their kiss was soft and quick, nothing like a sweeping romance scene, but when Melody stepped back, everything had changed forever.

CHAPTER 21
JANUARY 2000
MELODY

Each day in Melody's life passed more quickly than the last. Halfway through her third year of university now, she had been busy seeing Riley in her free time, of which there was none, but at least she got to sit with him in class. Melody liked him, and she knew he was way into her, but something kept holding her back from making a genuine commitment, so nine months later they were still just casually dating, and not for his lack of trying to take the next step.

There wasn't much time for friends outside of school, and it struck Melody as sad that even though Jack lived only a couple hours away now, they still barely saw each other. They had gotten together for a few hours just before school started again—not exactly the extensive visits over the summer they'd originally planned. She had hoped Jack being home in Ontario would give them more opportunities to spend time together, but they were both so busy.

What had improved, though, was their communication in-between visits. They were back to frequent letters and phone calls, and Melody's heart quickly healed from their lack of relationship while he was away. Jack was busy working and getting serious with Tanner, but Melody refused to have a repeat of 1995.

Thankfully, their schedules aligned, and she had time at the end of her winter break to travel to Tanner's house in Orillia for a quick visit with them both. When she arrived, Jack answered the door and pulled her in for a hug.

"Happy new year, Melody!"

It felt the same as it always had, like a reconnecting with a piece of herself that had been missing, however, the look on his face told her that something different hovered in the air between them.

"Come," Jack said, grabbing her hand and pulling her toward the back of the house.

"What's up?" Melody questioned, her heart beating faster.

"I had to tell you in person…" Jack paused and turned to face her. "Tanner had a key under the tree for me on Christmas morning. We're moving in together!"

Melody's initial reaction resembled sadness, but with Jack watching, she quickly changed her frown into a surprised smile.

"Wow, Jack! That's a massive step! I'm so happy for you both," Melody forced out, and leaned into him for a friendly side-hug as a distraction. "Does this mean you have to come out to your parents?"

"Yup. I'm not sure how they're going to take it, but it doesn't really matter. This is my life," Jack replied.

"Well, whatever happens, I am always here if you need to talk," Melody said, with a genuine hug this time.

Spring came quickly, and one rainy late-April morning Melody opened her mailbox and found a beautiful envelope with Jack's penmanship on the front. A slight numbness overcame her as she tore open the envelope, unsure what would be inside. To her relief, it was a piece of black cardstock with rainbow font at the top, requesting her presence at a 24th birthday bash for her best friend.

The date coincided with Riley's summer trip to BC to see family, so he would have to sit this one out. She hadn't even introduced him to Jack and Tanner yet, and it had reached that point where it had been too long and now it was getting awkward. Determined that slow and steady was the way to go with this relationship, Melody had avoided anything that would put her in a situation she wasn't emotionally ready for. *Like introducing my favourite person to my… favourite person?*

This would be her first time hanging out with Jack and Tanner since they started living together, which felt like a serious step in their relationship. Melody worried about how she'd handle it, but of course, she checked "yes" on the party RSVP card anyway and popped it in her bag to mail the next day. She didn't need to worry about that now.

Melody sat back down at her desk to get back to homework and studying. If only she could tuck her heartache away like the postcard in her bag. She made a mental note to call Jack the following day to gush with excitement, because that's what a good friend would do.

CHAPTER 22
JUNE 2000
MELODY

June 10th arrived with perfect weather, and Melody travelled north for the big day. Because she anticipated the party would be full of fabulous not-straight people, she had dressed up, doing her hair and makeup more enthusiastically than usual.

Jack and Tanner had spared no expense for this event, and Melody quickly theorized that it wasn't really a 24th birthday party—*who even has one of those*—so much as a coming out party.

Jack had spent many nights on the phone, agonizing over the parent situation with Melody. First, whether to tell them about Tanner, when things were still new—he didn't. And how to tell them things were serious, and they had moved in together—he did.

The information had created a monumental upheaval for his entire family, because of their beliefs, and when Jack called Melody with the details, she could feel his devastation through the phone. He said he couldn't confide in Tanner about this, as he didn't want Tanner to feel responsible for the rift in his family relationships. Jack also didn't want Tanner to doubt the decision, since Jack was essentially choosing between Tanner and his parents.

Melody reassured Jack that his gut instinct was what he had to trust. If this relationship with Tanner, which could potentially last his entire life, felt like everything he had dreamed of, then he couldn't let anything or anyone stand in his way. *Shouldn't I feel that way about Riley too? Why am I so disconnected?*

And so, on a beautiful June evening, Melody watched two of her friends celebrate their love, and Jack's birthday, as her chest cracked wide open. Her chipped and broken heart, overwhelmed by the shame and guilt of all her feelings in that moment, finally gave way. Refusing to make a scene, Melody went to the bathroom to pull herself together. Jack's parents already hadn't come, and though someday they would regret that choice, it was enough hurt for Jack to bear on his day.

Putting a cool rag on her neck and touching up her makeup, Melody tried to talk some sense into herself. *Girlfriend. This night is not about you, get yourself together. You owe it to Jack. You are here to celebrate him and support him.*

Melody returned to the hall, committed to enjoying the evening. It really was an awesome party—rainbow Christmas tree lights covered the room, a disco ball hung over the dance floor, and the bar offered specialized drinks in honour of her friends. Something pink and fruity with an umbrella for Tanner, and something brown and strong for Jack. The two were complete opposites, though they somehow complemented each other perfectly.

Midway through the night, after Melody lost count of how many drinks she'd had, she spotted someone in her periphery, giving a brief wave while mid-conversation. Melody turned to look and couldn't believe her eyes. *Cody!* She hadn't seen him since their impulsive road trip to London to help Piper, and unlike Jack, she hadn't kept in touch through the years. She waved back and planned to wait until he was done with his current conversation to make her way over to him.

Melody freshened up in the bathroom again and returned to

the bar for a drink. As she turned around, she found Cody standing right in front of her with a glass in hand.

"Cody!" she squealed and gave him an enormous hug, careful not to spill either of their drinks.

"Hey, Melody!"

"It's so good to see you! How many years has it been?"

"Almost six," Cody said with a pretend pout.

"Dang, where does the time go? What have you been up to?"

Cody shrugged. "Not a lot. I graduated high school by the skin of my teeth and I just finished college, studying business."

"That's great! I'm still in school, about to start my fourth year of psychology," Melody said.

"Wow. What made you take psych?" Cody asked.

"Uh, a lot of things, but mostly Piper. She really changed my life, as weird as that sounds. I haven't talked to her in all this time either, but here I am building a career based on those few months she played a role in my life."

"Ditto. I've been thinking about her a lot, actually," Cody began. "I have no idea where she is. I tried calling her grandma's house a few times, but she never answered, and I didn't want to just leave a message out of nowhere."

Melody nodded.

"Should we track her down? I still feel bad that we sent her off to the hospital and then disappeared off the face of the earth," Cody said.

"Did we disappear off the face of the earth, or did she?" Melody wondered aloud.

Cody shrugged. "I tried to send her a few letters too, but never received a reply. I have no clue if I sent them to the right place, though," he said, and he threw back his drink.

"Me too. I sent them to her grandma's. They might not live there anymore. Or it's possible she wants nothing to do with us."

"Maybe, but we could try to find her. Perhaps she's been wanting to find us too?"

"She knows our names and cities, she could have looked up our parents. We're not transient like her. I do hope she's okay," Melody said.

"Me too. I'm tired of wondering, though. Let's find out. Give me your number, before I'm too sloshed to remember to ask for it later, and we'll figure this out." Cody handed Melody a napkin from the bar top, and ordered another drink.

In an unexpected turn of events, the night was more fun than Melody predicted, after fighting off her breakdown earlier. She drank too much and danced for hours, and took all kinds of photos with Cody, Jack, and Tanner, and the few other Sweet Clover people who were there.

She had wondered if her "basic drunk girl crying in the bathroom" would come out over seeing her best friend, who she once thought might be more than that, celebrate his birthday with the man of his dreams on his arm. But that girl never emerged. Instead, she threw her arms around them both in a sweaty hug.

"I'm so happy for you both! Happy birthday Jacky-boy!" Melody shouted a little too loudly.

They both squeezed her and rolled their eyes at her sloppiness.

Tanner's speciality drinks must have had some magic in those little paper umbrellas, because Melody woke up the next morning without a hangover in her over the top hotel bed. She had splurged, because how often does your favourite person turn 24-years-old and come out to the world all in one night?

Melody journaled out her gratitude list, goals, and the morning's feelings, like she did every day. Part of being a psych major meant being obsessively involved with her own mental and emotional health and trying to work through issues before they even got to the surface, because she was way too aware what the alternative was, and last night had been a lot.

> Dear Diary,
>
> Jack's party was last night. I feared how I might handle it all, but instead of diving off the edge of an emotional cliff that would have led into a full-blown breakdown, I took a step back and had a lot of fun. Cody was there. We're going to find Piper. Isn't that wild?
>
> He has tried sending letters over the years too, but never got a reply. I am worried we won't find her, or what else we might learn along the way, but I need to try. Piper is such a loose thread in my life, like something more should have come from those intense few months of... would you call that friendship? I don't think so. However, we're going to try to reconnect with her. He's going to call me this week so we can plan our mission.
>
> I'm not sure how I escaped last night without a hangover. I was drinking away my feelings, and thankfully, it worked, and I didn't turn into a mess. Despite my own confusion, Jack's happiness is all that matters. If that is with Tanner, then I'm thrilled for them. Oh, and I am calling them TJ now. They are one. Haha. I'm relieved Jack has come out to the world and can finally be himself too. Things are rough with his family, and I will be there for him through that, but last night was a bit of closure for me, and maybe I'll be able to move on.
>
> I mean, I have Riley, so "moving on" isn't the right term. I shouldn't be moving on from something that

never existed in the first place, especially when something else already exists. But I am confused where I'm at with him and need to figure some things out. Ugh.
Melody

Melody checked her watch and realized she had to meet TJ for brunch in half an hour—something they'd decided after many drinks the night before. She hauled herself out of the duvet's warmth and retreated to the bathroom to make herself presentable.

She assumed they would have invited a few other people to join them that morning, but they hadn't. The meal only included the three of them. Melody gushed about how perfect the night turned out, Jack whined about how hungover he was, and Tanner, in typical fashion, shovelled food into his mouth faster than they could bring it.

After eating way too much, they sat chatting, and Melody shared her conversation with Cody and their plan to track down Piper.

"He has mentioned her a handful of times over the years. It seems like he never got over her," Tanner said.

"That's what it seemed like when we spoke last night too, though I wasn't sure how much had come to the surface because the mix of company and drinks made for some nostalgia," Melody said.

"Nah, it's probably how he truly feels. He has barely dated. What a tragedy for a guy that cute," Tanner began, "he's likely been pining for her this whole time."

They continued to gossip about the potential outcomes of finding Piper as they enjoyed the bittersweet tang of their grapefruit mimosas, but none of them could have guessed what would transpire a short ways down the road.

A few days after returning home from Orillia, Melody got a call from Cody. They brainstormed where Piper might be, avoiding the devastating option that neither of them wanted to discuss.

"Her grandma's house," Melody started.

"The hospital," Cody added.

"Let's not go there just yet. A foster home?"

"She would have aged out by now. Maybe with her mom?"

"I guess things might have gotten better on their own, though that's not very realistic," Melody said gently, trying not to upset him.

Though the list was short, they felt certain they hadn't missed any possibilities. They planned to start with calling Piper's grandma's house, since they already had that phone number and it would be the easiest jumping off point. Melody offered to make the call, since Piper's grandma might open up to a woman more easily than a strange man.

Melody picked the phone up from the receiver multiple times and re-cradled it each time. She wasn't sure why her nerves were ramping up; it had been a long time since she had such an aversion to phone calls. She figured it was her anxiety about what would happen if Piper wasn't at her grandma's. After half a dozen times around this circle, Melody dialled the number that Cody had given her and listened to it ring.

"Hello?" a raspy voice said.

"Hello, is this Piper's grandma?" Melody asked in her sweetest phone voice.

"…Yes?" the voice sounded uncertain, as if she did not want this conversation to continue.

Melody jumped at her chance. "Hi, it's Melody. I'm not sure if you remember me. I stayed at your house once when I came to visit Piper."

"Yes, yes, I remember. You came with all those young men. That was quite a fright for me at dawn."

Melody relaxed and held back a giggle. "Yes, I'm sure that must have been! I am calling to see if Piper is there? Or if you have any idea where she is? We lost touch and I don't have her address or phone number."

Piper's grandma cleared her throat. "Well, I don't know where Piper is. I dropped her off at the hospital that day after you all left, and then my life went to hell in a hand-basket in the weeks that followed."

She paused long enough for Melody to wonder if she should brace for bad news.

Piper's grandma continued. "They sent her back to foster care when she got out. She came back once, after something happened to her in one of those homes, however, I was still in a bad way, so I took her back to CPS. I guess she never forgave me for that, because I haven't heard from her in years. I wish I had an idea, or could be sure that I made the right choice, but I was desperate."

Melody heard the sorrow and regret in Piper's grandma's voice.

"I'm so sorry you have been having a rough time," Melody offered. "I will keep in touch if I find out anything about Piper. Can I leave you my number in case you hear from her?"

"Yes," Piper's grandma replied, and Melody heard the shuffling paper. She gave the number out slowly.

"Okay. And Melody? If you find her, please tell her I'm sorry and I love her."

Melody hung up, very disappointed, despite having discussed this potential outcome with Cody in advance. Now understanding this likely wouldn't be a straightforward task, she picked the phone up again and called him back.

"How doesn't her grandma know where she is? Doesn't that seem just awful to you? How can you not care about your family?" Cody's voice bordered on a yell.

"I know, Cody. But let's focus on the things we can control. Who should we call next?"

"CPS?"

"Okay. We obviously can't ask for her location, but hopefully we can at least find out if Piper is still living in a foster home. Though, that's unlikely at 22 years old," Melody explained.

Again, they decided Melody should call. Since Piper's dad had been such an awful guy, they didn't want to spook the caseworker when they called. Melody's hands were sweaty this time as picked up the phone. She scanned through the phone book, and called the CPS office closest to Piper's grandma's house.

"Hi, my name is Melody Burton. I am looking for a friend, Piper Shepard, that I lost touch with a few years ago. Her grandma told me that the last update she had was that Piper lived in foster care through your agency. I assume you can't tell me her whereabouts, but what about if she is even still in a foster home, or where foster kids typically go since she would have aged out already?"

The caseworker replied, "I can't release information about any individual. We also don't keep records accessible in the office past the time individuals leave our care, which is usually when they turn eighteen."

"Can you tell me, where would someone that's left the system go?" Melody asked.

"Unfortunately, many children who can't stay in foster care end up on the street. Some go back to their biological families, which can often be more dangerous than the street. Very few find a shelter to stay in, and even fewer end up with jobs that can support them in having their own homes," the caseworker replied.

"Okay, well thank you for the information, I appreciate it," Melody said before hanging up.

She dialled Cody again and relayed what she had learned. Cody's frustration and worry overcame him, and he sniffled into the phone. Melody imagined being back in the Fraser Bunkie, soothing him.

"I spent so many years trying to push my feelings for her out of my head, trying to move on. Now that we're attempting to find her, it's like no time has passed. I miss her so much."

Melody reassured him they would keep looking until they found her, and that she had a plan.

"I am going to keep making phone calls, but I want you to make a list of all the high schools in her area that she could have ended up at, and I am going to see if one of the school staff will give me any information."

It was a long shot. Like CPS, the schools were in the business of keeping children safe, not giving their information out to strangers on the phone, but they planned for Cody to do some sleuthing while Melody worked, and he would call her later that evening.

When Cody called after six o'clock, Melody jumped to answer it. Despite a hopeful attitude, it had been years, and they weren't sure if Piper was alive, or if she had moved across the country, or if she'd been homeless all that time. So much could change in almost six years.

"I need to find her," Cody said before Melody even greeted him.

"I know, Cody," Melody responded. "What did you find out today?"

"Nothing! No one even answered."

Cody's voice oozed disappointment during their call together, and everything Melody suggested was met with frustration. If there was no one at the schools, this meant they would have to wait until the second week of September if they wanted to find anything out from them. They continued brainstorming ways to find her.

"Hey, I have a wild idea. When's your next free day?" Cody asked.

"Friday and Saturday," Melody answered, "why?"

"Let's drive out to London and we can try to locate her with our boots on the ground, instead of trying to make all these calls. Especially if she's been living on the street; walking around looking for her would be the only way to find her, right?" Cody quipped.

"You're always up for a road trip, eh, Cody?" Melody laughed.

"Always. So, how about it?" Cody asked again, more excited this time.

"Okay, I guess you're right. Looking in person might be faster than this game of telephone tag. But let's go prepared. Let's mark a map with all the places we might find her, like the mall, if she has a job? And we can see if there are any shelters? What about the rougher areas of town where we may find homeless communities?"

"Yes," Cody said, writing a list as she spoke. "I have a map here. I'll do that."

"Perfect," Melody said.

"So, I'll pick you up at ten o'clock on Friday, okay?" Cody asked.

"Okay, I'll see you soon," Melody confirmed.

She hadn't realized how badly Cody wanted to make this happen. Melody's motivation was unclear. Closure on everything that happened maybe, though she wasn't as hopeful as Cody that they would actually find Piper. *The plan might prove a total waste of time, or it might be exactly what we need to do to find Piper. Either way, it will be an adventure.*

Melody worried they might find themselves in some precarious situations while they were in London, so she started making a list of things to pack:

- *Quarters for pay phones*
- *An extra map in case Cody's writing made his illegible*
- *Spare food to give to people on the street*
- *Cash to use for food and gas*
- *Overnight supplies, because it wouldn't be a quick trip*
- *A phone book to find a hotel or other amenities*

Melody nodded in confidence as she reread her list. She had another two days to pack and decide what else she should bring, so for now, she would start gathering these supplies. She made a mental note to call Cody on Thursday and tell him everything she'd packed. With adequate preparation, Melody hoped they'd find success on their trip.

The next thing to do was to tell Riley. They'd been together for over a year now, but Melody still considered it casual. They weren't living together, and they hadn't even said, "I love you". Well, she hadn't. Melody had thirteen-foot-high walls built around her heart. Riley adored her, and she probably wasn't being fair to him. Regardless of how unserious she perceived their relationship to be, however, her running across the province with a guy Riley had never even heard much about was presumably going to be met with some strong opinions. She took a deep breath and dialled his number.

"Hi. How's it going?"

"Hey! I just got off work. Do you want to go get some dinner?" he asked with golden retriever energy.

Melody's heart sank. "I would love to, but I'm busy packing for a trip. I am heading out to London on Friday."

"Oh? For what?" Riley asked.

"I'm meeting up with my friend Cody from camp, and we're going to find our friend Piper." *Their friend? She is Cody's ex, and my… life-altering acquaintance at best.*

"You're going to London with Cody for the weekend?" Riley's tone of voice told Melody everything she needed to know.

"It sounds odd, but I promise, it's not. Cody is harmless, Piper is his ex that he's still in love with, that's why we're going to find her." She paused for a response, but there wasn't one. "So, I'll call you when I get home, okay?"

Riley sighed through the receiver. "Okay, I guess I'll talk to you in a few days. Be safe," he said, and hung up the phone.

CHAPTER 24
JUNE 2000
MELODY

Friday morning arrived, and Melody was desperate to get going. She packed, double-checked, and repacked her bag multiple times, then resorted to pacing. Cody would be there at ten o'clock, and Melody had reached her limit by just after eight. She then gathered some snacks and drinks to make as few stops as possible, and to spend as little money as possible. This trip would be expensive enough with a potential motel stay.

Cody arrived early, which finally allowed Melody to stop pacing. The ride started a little rocky, as the two of them had never really spent any time alone together, at least not without multiple drinks involved, so Melody was quiet and awkward. Thankfully, Cody eventually took point in the conversation and started asking her questions about school—Melody's favourite subject.

The conversation flowed more easily as the drive progressed, each of them becoming more comfortable. They reminisced about the party, and how wild it was to have friends mature enough to be living together, and finally broached the subject of what the actual plan was when they got to London, and what would happen if they found Piper.

"Cody, will she want to see us after all these years?" Melody asked. "I mean, the party reconnected us, and it makes sense we want to find her now. But will it make sense to her?"

"It doesn't matter at this point. I need to do this," Cody admitted. "At the beginning, I found it easy to push my thoughts of her out of my head. I was trying to finish high school, playing football, going to lots of parties, and having fun fooling around with girls. However, the older I got, the less I wanted to be distracted by any of those things, and the more the feelings kept creeping back in. I've felt guilty for years about how things ended. I want a do-over."

Melody nodded, but stayed silent.

After a few hours on the road, they reached London. They stopped for a bathroom break and some coffee, and took the time to look at their map and Cody's list of locations. They started downtown, wanting to eliminate one of the more difficult searches first. The houses had boarded-up windows, broken down porches, and graffiti everywhere. It wasn't like anything that Melody or Cody were used to, living in quiet, middle-class, suburban neighbourhoods.

Cody had suggested ahead of time that they not get out of the car during this portion of their search. The pair understood their limitations in an unfamiliar situation, so they watched from their car windows for anyone resembling Piper. They passed alleys with tarp houses, and people on corners with signs asking for help. They drove by an entire tent community in the very deepest corner of downtown, which they avoided, but no signs of Piper. *What a relief.*

Melody suggested they check the shelters next. She figured that would be the next most difficult search location, and she wanted to check it off the list. Cody found three women's shelters, so they started with the closest and worked their way out. They had no experience with shelters, but assumed the staff would also be tight-lipped about their residents. They wondered if it would make more sense to wait outside and ask someone going in or out if they knew Piper instead.

The first shelter stood only a few blocks from the tent community they had passed, so when they parked outside on the street, they weren't at all surprised to see similar people heading in and out. Even with what little information they had about Piper now, they couldn't imagine, or didn't want to imagine, her living in a place like that, so they tried the next shelter instead.

Cody and Melody pulled up in front of The Rose Project not far outside the suburbs of London and looked at each other like they sensed something different here. The pale pink building looked friendly and inviting. Their sign was newer and seemed welcoming, listing the various services they provided. There were also several young women hanging around outside; chatting, playing basketball and watching kids drawing with sidewalk chalk. Melody let herself become hopeful for the first time on their trip. She was unsure what caused her to be drawn to this place, but she felt Piper was there.

They decided that, like the phone calls, they would have better luck if Melody started the conversations. Cody parked at the end of the lot, and Melody hopped out of the car. She approached a group of women sitting on a picnic bench, as they looked at her with narrowed eyes.

Melody took a deep breath. "Hi. I'm looking for my friend, and I wondered if she might be here. Do any of you know someone named Piper?"

The women all looked at each other as if trying to gauge if they should trust Melody. Expecting this might be a tricky situation, Melody had brought backup—a photograph they had taken of the five of them when they visited Piper's grandma's house. She inched forward to hand it to one woman.

"That's Piper in the middle. We lost touch after this photograph, and my friend Cody and I are trying to reconnect with her."

Melody pointed towards the car and Cody waved out the window.

The women again looked between themselves before one of them spoke.

"What's your name?" she asked.

"Melody. I am a friend of Piper's from camp."

The women changed their postures, and all relaxed at once.

"We know Piper. She's not here right now, but if you come back around dinnertime, you should be able to find her. We'll tell her you were here."

Their words still conveyed apprehension, though their attitudes seemed friendlier. This was the best she could hope for in this situation. It relieved her they had found success in their search, and so quickly too. They hadn't seen Piper yet, but they had a solid lead; a better outcome than Melody expected.

"Thank you, thank you so much!" Melody reached for the photograph and ran back to the car.

She pulled the door open with such force that Cody protested, "easy on the lady, she's not used to being jerked around!"

She explained the entire conversation with the women to him and watched as his smile grew bigger with each passing word.

"Yes! We did it!" Cody shouted and wrapped his arms around Melody when she finished the recap.

They left to grab a bite to eat to pass the afternoon, but their queasy stomachs wanted for nothing, and they ended up back at the shelter way earlier than they should have. They wandered around the block, enjoying the sunshine and fresh air, and hoping they might catch Piper on her way to The Rose Project, instead of having to find her after she'd already gone in.

The pair lost count of the number of laps they'd done, but after at least half a dozen, they spotted a young woman walking up the street towards them. Cody sped up and confirmed, with his eyes that worked much better than Melody's, that it was indeed Piper.

"Piper?" he called out.

She stopped in her tracks but didn't reply.

"Piper?" he called again as they got closer.

Piper must have connected the dots and figured out it was Cody calling her name. Her eyebrows shot up and her mouth gaped open.

"Cody?" her voice wavered as she said his name aloud, maybe for the first time in years.

He ran to her. He stopped mere inches away and let her make the next move. She threw her arms around him like a Hollywood romance scene, crying, quietly at first and then full-blown sobs. Melody caught up to the pair, and she saw that Cody too, had tears streaming down his cheeks. She stood back and waited.

After an embrace long enough to span over half a decade of distance, Cody pulled back from the hug and looked Piper in the eyes.

"Piper!" Cody said again, this time a statement instead of a question.

She beamed at him and then realized they weren't alone.

"Melody?" she asked, cocking her head to the side as if trying to make sense of the situation unfurling before her eyes.

"Hi, Piper," Melody said.

Piper stepped past Cody and wrapped her arms around Melody, but didn't say a word.

Melody squeezed her and moved backwards. "Piper, you look incredible!"

Piper blushed. Her shiny hair was curled and flowed down her back like a mermaid. She wore a light touch of makeup, little enough that you would second guess if it was there at all. It just accentuated her natural beauty. She'd come a long way from the pale, frantic looking teenager they'd seen all those years before.

"What are you doing here? How did you find me?" Piper asked.

"Well, it's kind of a long story..." Cody began.

"Have you eaten? Why don't you come in? I can show you The Rose Project."

Melody and Cody looked at each other but nodded in unison. They weren't sure what to expect when they stepped inside of the downtown London shelter, however, it didn't take long for them to realize it wasn't what they expected.

Cody and Melody followed Piper into the building and took in all the sights. There were bedrooms lined with multiple bunk beds, and a thunder of chatter and screeching chairs came from the far end of the hall.

Piper pushed open two large double doors to reveal a gymnasium filled with tables. Many women and children were already eating, and there was a long line up to the serving table. Melody struggled to imagine Piper living here, with so many people and no support.

Melody's opinion changed, however, when the residents noticed Piper come through the door, and all at once, they started shouting, "Piper!"

She wasn't without support after all. Piper ushered them over to a table and told them to wait. She walked to the front of the room and stood up on a chair to better see all the faces.

"Good evening, Roses, I hope you will enjoy the delicious meal we have provided by," Piper looked down at a piece of paper in her hands, "IGA, this evening! We will have our usual doors-open policy this weekend. If you're in touch with anyone who needs a hot meal, please bring them over. Unfortunately, we still don't have any empty beds available for new residents, but I'm sure that some of you are almost ready to leave us and make your own way in the world, and we are so proud of you! Happy Friday everyone, there will be games here in the gym after dinner."

Melody and Cody stared in shock. Piper wandered back over to the table she'd left them at and sat down. She started speaking before either of them could ask questions.

"I lived here for about three years. However, I'm no longer a patron. I work here. I am the night manager," Piper explained.

"Do you still live in the building?" Melody asked.

"No, not since I started working here. I have a small apartment nearby. It helps give the residents hope that change is possible, and the future is theirs for the taking. We pride ourselves on helping our residents make progress while they stay here, and eventually leave us for a successful life when they are ready."

"Wow, that's so great, Piper. I'm glad to see you doing so well," Cody said.

"Are you?" Piper's tone changed, making the hair on Melody's neck stand up. Her gaze narrowed on Cody. "Because it's been years and you're just coming to look for me now? Now when I'm healthy and don't need any help? Where were you all this time, Cody?"

Melody looked between the two of them. "We tried a few times to contact you, Piper. Cody and I both sent letters to your grandma's house. How could we track you down any other way? Besides, we kind of assumed you were avoiding us. There was no way for us to know that you weren't living there, or what you had been through since we visited."

"You all abandoned me. You convinced me, and my grandma, that I needed to go back to the hospital, and then poof, you were all gone from my life," Piper continued.

"Well, if you want to play the blame game, Piper," Melody started, her frustration boiling over, "where were you all this time that you didn't contact us? Both of our parents still live in the same place with the same phone number. They would have led you to us with one quick phone call. Relationships are a two-way street."

"I lost everything between being in and out of the hospital, getting kicked out of my grandma's, and running for my life from abusive foster parents. My bad. I should have hunted you down and checked in amidst all of that, I guess. It's not like I was trying to stay alive or anything," Piper's sarcastic edge sharpened her words.

"This probably isn't a conversation you want to have in the middle of your workplace, Piper. I think we should go somewhere else," Cody whispered.

Piper didn't hesitate. She stood, stormed out of the gym and ducked in a door in the middle of the hallway. Melody and Cody trailed behind her. When they were all tucked into her tiny office, Piper shut the door behind them.

"I lived in hell for a long time," Piper continued, calmer now, "and it took me years to get my life back on track. I graduated high school a year and a half late because of how much hardship I endured. My mental health has been an uphill battle every day of my life. I took this job to help other young women like me, but the government keeps clawing back our funding and it's like I'm failing every one of them. Yet they see me as living the dream, having moved out of the shelter into an apartment, gotten a good job, and living my life with purpose. I feel like a fraud every single day because I can't give them half the support that I received over those three years."

"You've been dealing with so much, Piper. I'm sorry we haven't helped," Melody said, and Cody nodded.

"I'm sorry doesn't make up for all the time I've been out here on my own. Why are you even here? Why did you decide to find me now? I don't see the point!"

"We were looking for closure, I guess," Melody started, and realized she'd said the absolute wrong thing in this situation.

"Closure? Do you think I've ever received a single moment of closure in my life? Have I had closure that my dad beat my brother to a pulp, and he died weeks later? Or how about that my mom was an addict and she got together with my loser dad in the first place? Do I have closure for all the foster parents who abused me, or the men who assaulted me? What about the fact that my grandma drank her life away when I needed her most?" Piper spewed. "What could the two of you need closure for?"

After a long moment of silence, Melody spoke. "Seeing your lifeless body messed me up, Piper. Having to save you from a suicide attempt at fifteen is a trauma that will stay with me forever. You understand what trauma is like. If I get some closure, it will help my state of mind. I'm studying to be a psychologist and I..."

Piper flicked her eyes to Cody. "And you?"

Cody looked away. "I missed you. I wanted to find you, see how you were doing, and to have a proper goodbye. But you're right, I abandoned you in your time of need. I haven't been able to hold down a relationship during all these years and I needed to see you to sort some things out and apologize. I've been carrying so much guilt for so long."

"Well, how nice that you both came to find me after all this time to fix your own privileged lives. I haven't had time or the emotional capacity to even consider a relationship. Between school, work, therapy, and taking care of all those women you saw out there..." Piper trailed off.

"That wasn't what we meant," Melody explained. "It wasn't all about us. We were thinking about you too."

"If it had been about me too, it would have happened years ago!" Piper snapped, her face turning red and her eyes like daggers. Melody worried about her backsliding if they upset her much further. That was the last thing they wanted to do, but she wouldn't see their side of this situation now. Emotions were running too high.

"We should go, Melody..." Cody said as he nudged her leg.

"We're sorry we've upset you, Piper. It seems like you're doing well for yourself, and we didn't mean to intrude on your new life here. We are so proud of everything you've accomplished," Melody said without looking up from the floor.

Piper scoffed at her sentiments. "Okay, Miss Therapist, please don't patronize me."

"Come on," Melody said to Cody as she opened the door.

Cody reached for Piper's hand and looked her in the eyes. "I am so sorry I abandoned you. I never meant to hurt you. I wanted to help. Don't worry, I won't bother you again."

And with that, the two of them walked out of the room, and out of Piper's life, for good.

CHAPTER 25
JUNE 2000
MELODY

Cody walked back to the car in silence, but the slam of his door was deafening. Melody slipped in quietly so as not to interrupt his outburst. They had discussed different outcomes for this trip; however, Melody hadn't expected Piper's contempt and was having trouble processing it.

They drove in silence, letting the evening sink in, and bitterness came with it. They went to such great lengths to find Piper, and she didn't even care. She seemed so excited to see them initially. But really, she wanted to lecture them and chastise them for not being there earlier. It didn't feel fair. Melody tried to put on her professional hat and put herself in Piper's shoes after hearing how awful her life had been, though it was still difficult to look past her own hurt.

Melody's anxiety kicked in the minute things got heated with Piper, and now it taunted her with all the things she should have said and all the ways she could have made the situation better if she wasn't so worked up. Then Cody's face screwed up in visible anger, like a cartoon character about to blow steam out of their ears. He turned to Melody and ranted until the steam had dissipated, and he finally cooled off.

"What if I was supposed to stick it out with her, what if we were supposed to be together forever, what if I had helped her instead of sending her to the hospital, what if I could have found her and rekindled our relationship, what if..."

The questions were rhetorical, and Melody stayed quiet. She only spoke to suggest they skip the motel and drive straight home, considering how early they were back on the road. Cody must have agreed because he just kept driving.

When they reached the halfway point, Melody asked Cody to make a pit-stop. He sighed without replying, before pulling off at the next exit. Now it seemed like Cody was frustrated with Melody too, and she wondered if she'd done more wrong than she was aware of. Her nerves, which had settled down during the long drive, kicked back into high-gear and she wrung her hands as they shook while she walked to the rest stop bathroom.

What have I done to upset Cody further? Am I selfish for waiting this long to search for Piper? How have I messed things up so badly when I have literal years of education in mental health and trauma?

The day had not gone as planned, and Melody wanted to take it back. By the time she returned to the car, she was gasping for air. Her body vibrated uncontrollably, and Cody took one look at her and wrapped his arms around her.

"It's okay," he whispered as he rubbed her back. "Just forget it."

But Melody couldn't. Piper played a part in her story. A huge part. She was the reason Melody studied psychology. But Piper was also a constant trigger, a nagging presence always in the back of Melody's mind that never went away. Every time Melody drove by a hospital, she thought of Piper, wondering where she lived and if she was okay. *Why did everything go so wrong?*

It took quite some time for Melody's breathing to slow and her tears to dry, but when they did, Cody let her go and adjusted in his seat.

"Ready?" he asked.

Melody nodded as she clicked her seatbelt into place. Cody shifted the car into drive and pulled out of the parking lot. She was embarrassed, and he was obviously unsure what to say, so the drive was awkwardly silent again. *How many times am I going to have a literal panic attack in front of camp guys? I haven't had one since that day at the jumping rocks with Jack. Am I just triggered by anything to do with camp?*

Cody dropped Melody off at home just after eleven o'clock. Neither of them was prepared to end their trip after the turn it took, and both sat there awkwardly. Melody didn't feel comfortable sending Cody on his way to drive home alone, stewing in his resentment.

"Do you want to come in for a bit? You still have such a long drive ahead of you," Melody offered.

"No, I'm okay. I just want to get home and go to bed," Cody said.

Melody nodded in understanding.

She gave him a quick hug and stepped out of the car. She waved to Cody, and he fiddled with the stereo before backing out of the driveway. Melody noticed the mail flag up, so she crossed the driveway and opened the mailbox. She turned around and waved to stop him from pulling away.

"Cody, wait!" she whisper-yelled, remembering what time it was.

Melody was holding a white envelope addressed to her, but the important part was where the envelope had come from— Camp Sweet Clover. Cody pulled back into the driveway and she tore open the envelope. He climbed out of the car to look over Melody's shoulder.

> *Dear Sweet Clover Staff & Volunteer Alumni,*
>
> *Please accept this invitation to a camp reunion this August 26–28, 2000. Enjoy a long weekend back at Sweet Clover, where you and your friends can reserve a cabin for yourselves, and come experience all the fun and beauty of our incredible camp again. Please call the camp office to RSVP and reserve your cabin right away so you don't miss out.*
>
> *Have a sweet day!*

"A reunion? We get to go back?" Melody squealed.

A huge smile crossed Cody's face, "This is such great news! I miss Sweet Clover so much!"

"I'm so happy I could cry!" Melody whispered.

Melody read the letter again to make sure she hadn't missed any pertinent details.

"We have to call first thing in the morning. We can share a cabin with Jack and Tanner," Melody said.

"Yeah, that sounds great," Cody started, "as long as there are no escapades… if you know what I mean." They both laughed until they were on the verge of tears.

With the dark cloud of their day dissipating, the two said their goodbyes with a longer hug, and parted ways in happier moods.

Melody watched Cody back out of the driveway, and then retreated upstairs, pulled out her calendar, and counted the days until camp. She jumped around her room and held back excited screams about going back to her favourite place.

Remembering how late it was, Melody took a quick shower and collapsed into bed. Frustrated and anxious thoughts still gathered in the back of her mind, but she was determined not to let them ruin her excitement.

It took Melody forever to fall asleep, and she woke up again at the crack of dawn, eager to call and get their cabin reservation in. She hadn't yet spoken to Jack and Tanner, but she assumed they'd be in. The moment eight o'clock struck, she dialled Camp Sweet Clover.

"Good morning, Camp Sweet Clover," a voice on the other end answered.

"Good morning! This is Melody Burton. I'd like to reserve a cabin for the weekend reunion, please!" she exclaimed way too enthusiastically for the early hours of a Saturday morning.

"Oh, yes, Melody, and who will bunk with you?" the voice asked.

"Jack Wilder, Richard Tanner, and Cody Hughes." Melody listed the names off as quickly as her mouth moved.

"That's quite the entourage of young men you have there. Did you have a cabin preference?" the camp staff asked.

"Oh yes, could we stay in Marigolds please? That would be incredible!" Melody responded. She stayed in the Marigolds cabin for the two years as a camper at Sweet Clover, and it would be so fun to stay there again.

"Yes, we can make that work. Okay, you're all set. We'll see you on the 28th!" The voice tried to match Melody's enthusiasm and failed.

"Oh, thank you!" Melody said before hanging up.

With the booking complete, Melody only had to connect with TJ. They wouldn't be awake yet though, so she sauntered downstairs to make some breakfast while she waited.

Sunshine poured in the kitchen windows. Melody put bread in the toaster and poured the cup of coffee that was brewed and waiting for her—*thanks past-me*—into her favourite mug and walked out the French doors onto the deck. The day was already blazing hot as Melody let the sun warm her outsides so they matched her insides. She imagined being young again, like the world was full of possibility. She wondered what she should spend her day doing, now that she was unexpectedly home. She started by calling Riley, he was usually up by now.

They spoke for a few minutes. He had the day off too, so they decided that a beach day was in order. Melody held back all the things she wanted to explain to him from the last 24 hours, aware that she could tell him in person soon. Instead, they made plans, and Melody hung up to go get ready. They never had a free day together, and it would be nice to have a date in the perfect weather. Melody hadn't made any realizations about her hesitation with their relationship, or what she should do about it. *Maybe today will help me figure it out?*

She needed to do one more thing before she got ready for the day—call TJ. She dialled their number and waited as it rang half a dozen times.

"Hello?" a groggy man-voice whispered into the receiver.

"Hey, it's Melody. I'm sorry, did I wake you?"

"Sort of. It's okay though. What's up?" She now recognized the voice as Tanner's.

"Did you guys get the mail yesterday?" she asked.

"Uhhh, no, I guess not," Tanner mumbled.

"Go get it, and call me after, k?" she said.

"Okay, Mel," he grumbled. Tanner was the only person who called her Mel, but she liked the way it sounded coming from him.

"Jack! Go get the mail and call Melody back!" she heard Tanner yell before he hung up the phone.

It took forever for Jack to call her back. She had already gotten dressed and done her hair in the time between the calls. When the phone rang, she didn't even say hello, but sprang right into her enthusiastic rambling.

"Isn't this so great? I already reserved a cabin for the four of us. You guys are good to go, right? Cody's already confirmed, and he's stoked. Are you guys stoked?" She stopped for a breath.

"Yes," Jack answered to all the questions at once, not as energetic as Melody this morning. "Is Riley coming?"

"Um... good question," Melody responded, wondering how she'd forgotten this minor detail. "I think if it's for alumni, it should just be us?"

"Sure thing," Jack said, with no discernible inflection in his tone.

Melody had been waiting for this. A chance to reclaim her camp memories from six years earlier, with something real. Why did it feel like the time between camp visits was a purgatory, preventing her from living the life she longed for? What was going to happen when this weekend was over? She practically smelled the pine and lake air already, and she was ready to soak up every minute of camp life with three of her old friends.

She couldn't come up with a better way to end her summer if she tried.

CHAPTER 26
JUNE 2000
PIPER

Piper hadn't shared with anyone where she had been living all that time—not even her grandma. None of them cared, anyway. Even so, her stomach was sick with guilt, as she sat on her bed wondering what she should have done differently. Especially about how secretive she had been and how hard she had come down on Melody and Cody. They were right; she decided at last. It was a two-way street, and she hadn't done her part either. For all she knew, they worried about her constantly.

The only place she had kept updated with her address, ironically, was CSC when she had moved to her new apartment. She was hoping to reconnect with the staff there and setup a program for the teen residents at The Rose, so that had been her first step on a very long list—confirming that she still existed. *Yup, I had been doing just fine before my present got mixed up with my past.*

Piper pulled the leather-bound journal out of her desk and started a new page with the date at the top, like she always did.

On Monday, June 19th, three days after Melody and Cody's visit, Piper opened her apartment mail slot to find an envelope with a handwritten address, which surprised her because her mail was only ever bills. She stared at the writing, trying to decipher the sender before she flipped over the envelope to look at the return address. Camp Sweet Clover. Piper smiled with anticipation. She tore open the envelope right there in the foyer and leaned against the wall as she read it.

Her jaw dropped as she tried to piece everything together. *Is this for real? I have a chance to go back to camp? If I got the invite that would mean that Cody, Melody, Jack, and Tanner all would have too. Would they be going? I was a little ruthless. Maybe it isn't a good idea for me to go if they are going to be there. Would it be awkward? Who would I hang out with if we're all still mad at each other?*

It took her hours to sift through all the noise in her head. On one hand, it might trigger a past trauma, however, it could also be exactly what she needed for some closure. *There is that word again.* As soon as she'd formed that sentence in her mind, she realized she had pushed away the two people that cared enough to have sought her out, and for no good reason.

What she had to do was clear. Piper would go back and make peace with her camp friends, hoping to live a more open and healthy life. She kept commending herself for sticking with her meds, attending therapy, and working through her mental illness to become a healthier person, but did she actually feel healthy? If she was still hiding things from people, holding grudges, being hypocritical when she just admitted to wanting the same things, that wasn't healthy. She wasn't a therapist, but she'd been through enough sessions to know that she was still avoiding things that would help her heal.

How could she continue preaching about how to get better and lift yourself out of your situation to all the women and children at The Rose Project, when she had shied away from working through her own stuff? It was impossible; she decided. Something had to change.

The weeks between the invitation and the reunion dragged by. Piper had called the following afternoon and requested her old loft room, which seemed both super brave and incredibly stupid. She figured she would need access to the scene of the crime to process everything, and she couldn't do that if someone else inhabited that bedroom.

Finally, the morning of the 28th arrived. Victoria had graciously loaned Piper her car, so she didn't have to navigate a convoluted multi-bus trip all the way from London to the other end of the province and back three days later. Victoria had understood that this trip would act as a mental health pilgrimage, and had encouraged Piper to go through with it, even when her confidence wavered. And it did waver. The idea terrified Piper. The closer that morning had gotten, the louder her body protested with various aches. But she needed to go.

The drive to Camp Sweet Clover was peaceful, like it always had been when she was a child. Like she had left behind every bit of hurt and pain, and would be in a place where she felt more at home.

Leaving on a Friday morning and heading in the opposite direction of rush hour had turned out to be perfect timing, and she easily made it through Toronto which always stressed her out. Piper had only done a big drive like this a handful of times since she got her license, since she didn't have a car. When she got the job at The Rose Project though, she had to drive their van to take residents to appointments.

Piper made a quick pit-stop in Whitby for food and a bathroom, and got back on the road. She spent the last stretch of the drive giving herself a pep talk out loud. She planned out her return and how she would overcome her past and heal her future —an enormous task for a long weekend. As she tried to push down the panic that threatened to choke off her air, and the fear of rejection that blurred the road lines, she recognized that this was the only way to do it.

PART THREE
WILDFLOWERS

CHAPTER 27
AUGUST 2000
PIPER

It all started with a dip. Piper didn't even unload the car before she sprinted down the hill into the camp, past the dining hall and bunkie, and down the stairs to the waterfront. Her heart pounded with excitement and exertion now, not worry. Piper grinned as she ignored the lifeguard that called for her to stop running on the dock, and she sprinted to the end and dove off into the jet-black water. When she resurfaced a moment later, smelling the lake and the hundred-year-old pine trees, it was as though she had been reborn.

She embodied preteen Piper at summer camp again. Before things got so tumultuous at home, before her mental health went off the rails, before attempting a shortcut off the planet, before living in the hospital, before her brother's death, before her dad went to prison, before her grandma abandoned her, before adults who were supposed to protect her assaulted her, and before she moved alone and terrified into a shelter.

She was Piper again, for the first time in a decade, and she wasn't afraid. As she blinked reality back into focus, however, she remembered exactly what she had to accomplish that afternoon, and it all came rushing back. The fear, the need for an escape to avoid her pain, and the possibility of rejection.

The next step in her plan was terrifying—rebuilding her friendships. Piper had faith that Cody, Melody, Jack, and Tanner wouldn't miss such a great opportunity, even without a way to confirm it. This place embodied heaven on earth and held so many incredible memories for everyone who walked barefoot through the grounds. There was something magical at Camp Sweet Clover. Camp people seemed to hold the same power. They reconnect you to this place even when you're far away, at least, that's what she'd felt when Cody and Melody showed up in her everyday life. She suspected that feeling is what lead Cody and Melody to search her out after the years.

Piper hauled herself out of the lake, her heavy clothes protesting every second. She trudged back up the hill, taking it all in as she returned to Victoria's car to grab her bags. Piper hadn't thought through the discomfort of walking around in soaking wet clothes that clung to her skin in the August heat, but she didn't regret her choice one bit.

For the first time since 1994, Piper climbed the wooden stairs to her loft room in the bunkie to change, then she began her next task. With a dry outfit and an envelope addressed to her four friends, she ventured the least obvious way to the Marigolds cabin to deliver it unnoticed. Piper didn't even need to ask the office if that's where they were staying; she knew Melody well enough, despite their brief relationship, to deduce that she would want to be back in the cabin she stayed in as a camper, for the same reason Piper wanted to be in the loft bedroom.

She left the envelope on the first bunk inside the cabin and then snuck back out to implement the rest of her complicated strategy. It had required plenty of careful planning, and she thanked her past-self for taking the time to do that while she was still at home and not overwhelmed by the sounds and smells of CSC.

Piper walked the camp grounds and put each envelope and box in its proper place and returned to the bunkie, hoping no one would find her deposits. Now, all that she could do was wait.

Retreating to her room, Piper crawled into her sleeping bag on the thin, stiff camp mattress. Her brain was volleying thoughts of two distinct periods in time and all the hurt and healing between them. She laid in silence and let her body do the rest, inhaling the peace and happiness of the current moment, and exhaling the hurt and trauma of her memories. In her meditation, she drifted off to sleep.

Piper woke to the sound of the bell signalling the change from third to fourth session, for those following the typical camp schedule. She hadn't seen many people when she first arrived, but when she got up and looked out her window, plenty of young people milled about, talking amongst themselves, reuniting with long hugs and gigantic smiles.

Piper looked in the small mirror behind the door and fixed her ponytail before leaving the room. She wanted to get a backseat view of her plan unfolding, so she crept out the back door of the bunkie, snuck down various paths between buildings, and walked along the waterfront up to the back of the Marigolds cabin. The windows were already open, and she heard the conversation taking place inside.

"This is kind of weird. I'm not super comfortable with it," a male voice said.

"I came here intending to unpack some of my feelings about this whole situation, so I'd like to follow it through," a female voice, obviously Melody, replied.

"We understand you guys haven't seen her, and maybe haven't cared to in years, but we saw her, and we have been thinking about her all this time. I'm kind of messed up, honestly, and I need to do this," said another male voice. *Cody*.

"It's just another way for her to get attention. I watched her choices destroy you, Cody. It took you months to recover. I don't want you to have to pick up those pieces again," a third male voice replied. *Maybe Tanner?*

Piper's guts twisted again. She leaned against the cabin wall and let out a shuddering breath. *What I did was hurtful to others, that is obvious, but I didn't realize just how much of an impact it made on my friends. Were they right to disappear from my life? Maybe that's what they needed to heal. Can I really begrudge them for that? I have been wrong all along. For years, I've harboured pent-up bitterness, blaming them for my loneliness, but I guess I should have directed it at myself instead.*

Piper couldn't listen to any more of their conversation. She no longer felt worthy of them playing along with her plan, or that she deserved their forgiveness or their friendship. She shouldn't have come back to this place.

Sneaking off back towards the waterfront, Piper ran along the footpaths all the way around the grounds and through the forest until she reached the jumping rocks. She had had enough spontaneous swimming for one day, but she would find quiet there. She needed to reconsider this plan because she had an inkling it all might blow up in her face.

As soon as she stopped running, Piper's chest tightened, and her thoughts jostled around her brain at a mile a minute. Fight-or-flight mode engaged her body, and she was unprepared for these symptoms. As someone with bipolar, she had become used to battling extreme lows, including major depressive episodes and suicidal ideation, and extreme highs, including manic behaviour and impulsive decision making. However, the anxiety was new to her, and she hadn't ever had a panic attack that she recollected.

Piper had a lot of experience with panic attacks from working with her residents at The Rose, so she easily regurgitated practical coping mechanisms to herself, but it was different when it was her own brain. She now understood why people with anxiety were so quick to become overwhelmed and frustrated. The physical symptoms she was experiencing combined with the mental ones were unbearable.

Make it stop. Make it stop.

Piper sat down on a bed of pine needles, leaned her back against the rough bark of a massive tree, and stared out at the lake lapping against the shore. Focused on her breathing, she followed the pattern of the small waves crashing into the rocks below. Eventually her heartbeat slowed and her stomach stopped rolling, but her mind kept running in overdrive.

Should I leave? It might be better if they could collect the clues and see that I'm sorry, without having to face me, and me them. Maybe an apology is enough, and I can just disappear again. But what would all this have been for? What would be the point of taking three days off work, borrowing Victoria's car, driving all the way out here for this grand gesture, doing everything in my power to reconnect with them and then running away scared before hearing the outcome? The swirling in her head was debilitating. She had to snap out of it, but she wasn't sure how.

Piper stared at the water, still breathing with the movement. She tried to empty her mind and focus on her breath. It took a long time, but her sweating eventually slowed. Mostly calm again, she breathed a sigh of relief before she heard a twig snap behind her. It startled her enough that she sprung to her feet and started running again. She wasn't running in a panic this time, more because she likely looked like a hot mess, and probably smelled like one too. She wanted to get back to her bedroom and freshen up before she saw anyone.

Piper followed the wooded paths to the back door of the bunkie again. With no idea if any of the other rooms were being used, she crept inside and sprinted up the stairs. Changing her shirt for the second time that day, she chose her favourite tie dye one, put on another swipe of deodorant, ran a comb through her hair and put it back up in a ponytail, and used a makeup wipe on her face to freshen up.

It didn't feel like enough, but it would meet camp standards where no one donned makeup, and everyone just wore t-shirts, cut-off shorts, and don't forget the Birkenstocks. They might as well have been a part of the camp uniform. Piper had spent the weeks since she received the invite, hunting through the local thrift stores, looking for a pair just for this trip. She slipped hers on, took a quick look in the mirror, and left the room.

Piper wasn't sure what her next move should be, but she couldn't make it in her bedroom. She walked out using the front door this time and stood on the porch as she looked out over the centre of camp. The scene before her played out as perfectly as she remembered. Her nostalgia overtook her. She wasn't ready to leave yet.

Piper took a deep breath, put a smile on her face, and walked all the way to the north field to the hidden spot she used to meet Cody when they were sneaking around. Now for something simple; she would sit there and wait.

CHAPTER 28

AUGUST 2000
MELODY

Melody hadn't even considered the fact that making the drive to camp with Cody and TJ would be so reminiscent of their road trip to London all those years ago. It thrilled her to have the extra time with the guys, though something seemed to be bothering Cody. He remained silent most of the drive.

"Hey, Codes, you awake?" Tanner joked, looking in the rear-view mirror.

"Huh?" Cody responded.

The other three friends laughed, but he rolled his eyes with annoyance.

"We're almost there!" Melody squealed as they exited the highway and travelled north via the country back roads.

Of course, by "almost" Melody had meant they were still an hour south of Camp Sweet Clover, but it was close enough. Everyone's moods lifted, including Cody's, as Melody popped in her camp mix CD, and the four of them began to dance and drum. Soon they were all singing along, cruising, windows down, and waiting to get a hint of the unforgettable scent of camp.

The moment they pulled onto the dirt road, Melody remembered the first time she'd driven it with her parents, anxious about going to camp for the first time, and wondering if their old clunky van would make it out. And now, nine years later, she was experiencing it in TJ's brand new car with her longtime friends, expecting one of the most memorable weekends of her life.

The parking lot was half-full when they arrived after lunch. Melody, Cody, Tanner, and Jack unloaded the trunk that contained way too many bags for a three-night stay.

Walking down into the centre of camp was surreal. Melody kept taking deep breaths of the perfect camp air and looking around, watching for people she knew. The group trekked to the back corner of the camp and up the porch steps to the Marigolds cabin. Then scampered around the room to pick the bunks they wanted—Tanner and Jack opting for the two twin counsellor beds, which they could push together into a queen. Scandalous. *What was that joke Cody had made?* Melody giggled to herself.

They had redone the cabins, or at least their cabin, since the last time she was there. Brand new pine bunks lined the walls, providing enough beds for everyone—one for sleeping and one for unpacking. As Melody moved her bag to the mattress beside her, she noticed a white envelope. Because it lacked a name, she opened it. She had booked this cabin, so it must be for her if anyone, right? Inside, she found a handwritten note.

My friends,
    I thought I would find you here. I knew Melody couldn't pass up a weekend at her favourite place in the world, and I assumed that she'd want to relive her camp days in the Marigolds cabin. I also predicted she'd be able to talk you three guys into coming with her.
    You must be wondering what the purpose of

this letter is. I had a hard time planning how to apologize in a meaningful enough way or to regain your trust in me in the short span of a weekend, so I put together a few clues to show you how much you all mean to me, and I hope you will follow them.

Sincerely, Piper

Melody read through the letter twice before anyone noticed her stillness and silence.

"What's that?" Jack asked.

"It's a note… from Piper," Melody replied, shooting a hesitant look at Cody. His eyes widened. "Here," she said, offering it to him to read.

"This is kind of weird. I'm not super comfortable with it," Jack replied after reading the letter over Cody's shoulder.

"I came here intending to unpack some of my feelings about this whole situation, so I'd like to follow it through," Melody replied.

"We understand you guys haven't seen her, and maybe haven't cared to in years, but we saw her, and we have been thinking about her all this time. I'm kind of messed up, honestly, and I need to do this," Cody explained.

"It's just another way for her to get attention," Tanner said. "I watched her choices destroy you, Cody. It took you months to recover. I don't want you to have to pick up those pieces again."

"We need to do this," Melody pressed. "You guys don't have to if you don't want to, but Cody and I need to."

Cody nodded in agreement.

"We're here for you, whatever you need," Jack replied.

"Let's get this over with," Tanner added.

"Okay, are you ready, Cody?" Melody asked.

"Yup, let's do this."

Written on the back of the letter, they found the first clue:

Clue 1: If I Had a Boat.

"Wow, it's been years since I've heard Lyle Lovett," Jack said sarcastically, having just heard it in the car. "But what does it mean?"

Melody ran through the campfire song in her head.

"It could either be down at the waterfront where the boats are, or in the pony field where the horse barn used to be, or at any of the places we had sing-alongs," Melody concluded.

"It's the waterfront," Cody said.

"I'm not so sure," Tanner interrupted, "there are so many songs to do with boats and water. Why would she pick the one that references a pony, if it wasn't the pony field?"

The group agreed and hiked into the north field covered in long grasses and clovers, which once upon a time had been called the pony field. Luckily for them, Piper hadn't made this hunt too difficult. They saw a banner tied across the opening of the dilapidated barn that had tiny paper boats on it. Without hesitating, Cody and Melody took off. TJ caught up before they reached the barn. When they got there, they were all out of breath and smiling.

"I told you so," said Tanner.

"Okay, but where's the clue?" Jack asked.

"There!" Melody shouted, pointing at the horseshoes nailed to the wall. Piper had tucked the envelope behind a horseshoe and addressed it to "The Four". Tanner plucked it down and opened the envelope to read the note aloud.

I would first like to start with an apology to all of you, but Cody and Melody especially. I was a first-class bitch when you found me in London. I was taken-aback, and my emotions were going wild. Seeing you triggered me and brought back past trauma, so it was a tough time all around. I didn't handle it well, and I regret my behaviour. Will you forgive me?

On the back of the note, they found the next clue:

Clue 2: Jumper.

"Gosh," said Melody, "I have listened to that Third Eye Blind song a thousand times reminiscing about everything I went through with Piper. It's on my camp mix for that reason. How did she know?"

"Where is it leading to?" Cody asked her.

"Her bedroom in the Fraser Bunkie. I mean, that's where I saved her life, right?" Melody suggested.

The group nodded in agreement and walked all the way back to the centre of camp, Tanner huffing and puffing.

"This is my exercise for the day, geez."

They entered the bunkie and up the steep steps the girls shared that year. Melody stopped with her hand on the doorknob, realizing she was hyperventilating, and unlike Tanner, it wasn't from the exercise. The others lined up behind her, not understanding what she was waiting for.

"Melody?" Jack said from halfway down the stairs.

"I, uh…"

"It's okay," Cody said, putting a hand on her shoulder.

She turned to look at Jack, and he nodded, encouraging her to turn the knob. She sighed with relief as she found nothing of concern behind the door. The guys filed into Piper's room behind Melody, packed like sardines in the tight space. A suitcase sat on her bed, however, beyond that the room looked bare.

Melody glanced around. This clue was for her. She raised her gaze to the wood ceiling overhead and saw the envelope on the beam where Melody had swung down into the room. She gestured to Cody, the tallest, and he jumped and snatched it down. Addressed again to "The Four", Melody opened it and everyone read over her shoulder.

I'd also like to address my behaviour from years ago. Can you believe it's been that long since we've all been here together? My mental illness was undiagnosed and untreated, and the circumstances in my life were a complete disaster. I was drowning, and though I'm not sorry for what I did, because it wasn't something I could control, I want to apologize that you all had to experience that with me. Melody, you have suffered trauma from having to save my life, and I want to tell you I am so thankful every morning when I wake up and have a life to live. I acknowledge what you did every minute of every day.

Melody blinked furiously to keep the tears at bay. A perfectly written apology, and Piper even recognized Melody's burden.

That might have been the most important part to her. She cradled the note to her chest, and Jack wrapped his arm around her. She turned it over to find the third clue.

Clue 3: Just a Friend.

Jack and Melody both looked up into each other's eyes and burst out laughing. Cody and Tanner stared at them, confused.

"I don't understand how she knows about that song. We were the only ones there! I haven't even heard it since that day!" Jack said with a chuckle.

"That's only because we hadn't gotten to it yet on my camp mix," Melody said, smirking.

Jack took the stairs down two at a time, becoming a boy again and getting carried away, seeming to have found the fun in the hunt at last. He slowed down at the bottom just enough to grab Melody's hand, dragging her along as they sang together. Melody stopped on the bathroom porch, and he flung open the boy's door, returning with two envelopes. One envelope was for "The Three", and the other was for "Cody". He handed Cody his and opened the other. He read it aloud.

You all are doing an incredible job on this hunt. It was so much fun pulling camp-related songs from my soggy memory to use for the clues. I hope you can tell that my sentiments are heartfelt and that I am sorry, and grateful that you are even partaking in this. The time I spent alone brought about so much healing and growing, and I am truly happy now.

I hope the years have been kind to you too, and this weekend will help you all find closure and make new, fun camp memories.

On the back was clue four:

Clue 4: Say It Ain't So.

The answer came to Tanner before anyone else, "The dining hall! Remember, Jack? We did that talent show… gosh, it must have been when Melody and Piper were still campers, and we lip synced to Weezer!"

They all recalled the memory at once, smiling and nodding. They didn't move, however, instead they watched Cody as he stared at his envelope.

"You guys go ahead, I'm going to open this in private."

Tanner still didn't move. He looked to Cody, and then to Jack, who was waiting with Melody, ready for the next adventure.

"Tanner?" Jack said.

"I'm good, Tanner," Cody said, looking him in the eyes.

Tanner nodded and turned towards Jack and Melody, leaving Cody alone with his letter.

CHAPTER 29

AUGUST 2000

CODY

Cody stood frozen, worried what his note would say, or where it would lead him. Taking a deep breath, he tore the envelope open.

Cody,

I first want to tell you I am so sorry for the way I acted in London, and the awful mistake I made right here at camp. I'm sorry I lashed out at you for trying to get me the help I needed. It wasn't right for me to blame you for leaving me. You had an opportunity for a better life; I understand that now. My heart felt at home with you when we were together, something I had never experienced with someone before, and because of that, I missed you all these years.

Piper

Cody's eyes welled with tears as he reflected on her sentiments. He had always tried to put her to the back of his mind, but he too, had missed her this entire time. Cody had always wondered if she had been doing okay, and whether he had made a mistake by abandoning her at the hospital. If he was being honest, he had waited for this day, and that's why he'd never had success with any of his other relationships.

He flipped the note over and read the clue on the back:

Clue: Gin Blossoms.

At this, Cody's throat became full and his eyes overflowed. This song, their song. It was the one that he had played on the guitar for her countless times, especially on her bad days, before everything fell apart. It embodied true love for them. Cody remembered where they had been the first time he had played it and started walking in that direction, wiping the tears from his cheeks. They had been on their way back from the campfire, which is why he'd had his guitar with him, and they'd snuck off to a little lean-to in the forest.

When he arrived at the spot, to his surprise, Cody found the lean-to still stood there, and was, in fact, better constructed than it had been when they were teens, and he wondered whether the camp staff had done it or if she had. Crawling inside, he found a box with a drawing on the top—a badge with a broken heart on it. Cody closed his eyes and prepared himself for what might be in it, and removed the lid.

Inside, a stack of large black notebooks awaited him. He opened the top one and saw the first page addressed, "To Cody" dated August 22, 1994. It was a letter she'd written him from the hospital and never sent. He flipped the page, "To Cody", August 23, 1994, he flipped again, "To Cody", August 24, 1994.

Thumbing through dozens of pages, he reached the bottom of the box and pulled out the last book, and flipped to the last page.

> August 26, 2000
>
> To Cody,
>
> I wrote to you every day for six years. I didn't think I would ever see you again, and I never expected to give you this archive of letters. Some of them are heartbreaking, some of them are bitter, some of them exude hopefulness, but the thread throughout the stack of books is that I never stopped waiting for you. I have missed you every single day.
>
> I have no idea if you lived life the same way. Heck, you may already be engaged or married for all I know. We didn't get to do much talking in London. However, I could not let another day go by without giving these to you and apologizing for every heartache I caused you. I love you, always.
>
> Piper

Cody sobbed as he pictured Piper writing these letters to him for six years straight. There were thousands of letters. He became overwhelmed with emotions he couldn't name and thoughts he struggled to make sense of.

He sat in silence, waiting for the tears to stop flowing.

When Cody finally composed himself, which felt like it took forever, he started looking for Piper. He knew he'd find her in their other spot, tucked away behind the shed at the waterfront.

Because the waterfront closed after session four, it was always empty for hours at a time in the evening. It had been the perfect getaway for them, and no doubt he would find her there now.

What he was unsure of, however, was what he would say to her when he got there.

Cody followed the path to the shed and walked in behind it, where the foliage was so overgrown it threatened to wrap him up. Obviously, none of the counsellors from this season had been using this spot. *Maybe they don't even know about it.* He stepped back into the woods to a gathering of stumps and found Piper already sitting there waiting. Although he expected to find her there, the sight of her still made him jump.

"Piper," Cody said, breathless partially from his hike and partially from his swirling emotions.

"Hi, Cody," Piper said hesitantly.

"I can't believe you wrote to me every single day. And I can't believe you never sent a single one," Cody said as he walked towards her and sat down on the stump next to hers.

"I didn't want to bombard you with all my baggage if you really wanted to cut ties, like you said. It was hard to write them and not send them. I wanted to tell you," Piper explained.

"I wish you'd sent some. At least so I would have been aware that you were still thinking about me."

"In hindsight, I wish I had too, but when I finally felt stable enough for a relationship, we'd lost contact, and I was afraid that no reply, or returned mail, would be worse for my heart than not knowing."

"It's been a lot of years, Pipes. I have missed you so much," Cody nudged her playfully.

"You have? I wasn't sure if you'd even still care about me."

"I tried to tell you, back in London. I wanted to explain

everything, but you were so upset," Cody said, staring at the ground, digging his shoe in the dirt.

"A rush of triggering memories overwhelmed me. I'm sorry. The appropriate response would have been to ask for space and time to process before lashing out," Piper said, reaching for his hand.

"I forgive you," Cody replied, looking her in the eyes for the first time. "And I'm sorry too. For abandoning you, for not reaching out sooner."

"You forgive me?" she asked. "For everything or just London?"

"There isn't much else to forgive you for. You were going through a rough time, and you had like... medical stuff going on. You weren't trying to hurt me. Besides, I couldn't help you when you really needed it and then played the white knight trying to save you when you were healing and doing well in London. If anyone should apologize, it's me," Cody said.

Piper threw her arms around his neck and wrapped him in a tight hug. Cody froze, waiting for his mind to catch up with the pounding of his heart in his chest. Piper's scent filled his nose and her soft hands reached up to touch his face. She paused, looking him in the eyes.

Cody hesitated for half a second and then leaned in. The brush of her lips on his set off a chain reaction he couldn't stop. His right hand had entwined itself in her long ponytail cascading over her shoulders, and the other gripped her waist and pulled her in towards him, as if the sliver of space between their bodies was too much. He was where he belonged again.

Their embrace continued until they got spooked by a noise nearby. They both pulled away, startled for a moment, and then laughed together for the first time in years.

"Why are we scared? It's not like we are going against camp policy anymore," Cody said with a smirk.

"It's funny how quickly I time-traveled, imagining we were

back here for real, sneaking around," Piper giggled. "That's the second time that's happened to me today!"

Cody's eyes grew wide.

"Getting spooked by a noise in the forest, I mean!"

He laughed. "So, where do we go from here?"

"Well," Piper began, putting her professional work-voice on. "Let's talk about the logistics?"

"Okay," Cody nodded.

"I live in London."

"And I live in Belleville."

"It is over four hours apart," Piper said.

"But I drive, that's not that far away."

"Could we really make this work?"

"Maybe? After all this time, I think we owe it to ourselves to try, don't you? We haven't stopped wondering about each other after years with no contact," Cody said.

"Yes, you're right. There's no harm in trying. Well, I mean, it could be harmful, but the what ifs would be more detrimental to our lives if we didn't test it out. Lots of people do distance relationships, right? It can't be that hard…" Piper trailed off.

"Right." Cody said, not feeling very confident, though he was sure he wanted to try.

The pair stared at each other, neither knowing what to do now. Cody acted first. He grabbed Piper's hand.

"Walk with me."

They crunched through late-summer leaves on the forest floor and weaved their way through ancient trees down to the water. A light rain fell as they stood on the shoreline and watched the waves crash near their feet. It brought on that petrichor that Cody loved. He held the box of letters to his chest with his free arm, trying to prevent them from getting damp.

"I watched the water splash onto the shore a few hours ago, over at the jumping rocks. I was in the middle of a full-blown panic attack, not sure if you guys were going to follow my clues or if I was making a fool of myself and should take off before any of you saw me. It was the lowest I've been in a long time. I am so relieved that you trusted me with another chance. What about Melody, Tanner, and Jack, though? Did they follow the clues too? They must have, right? I made some clues specifically for them, so you wouldn't have known all the answers."

"Yes, they took part. In fact, they were off to find what I assume would be the last clue before I read my letter. I needed to have time on my own," Cody explained.

"I wonder how they're doing. Maybe it's time to go find them?"

"Yes, we've been MIA for long enough, and it's almost dinnertime," Cody said, looking at his watch, "so where was the last clue leading?"

"Come on, I'll show you," Piper replied with a huge smile, as she took his hand and led him along the waterfront back towards the centre of camp.

CHAPTER 30
AUGUST 2000
MELODY

Melody, Tanner, and Jack charged into the dining hall at full speed, fighting to get through the door first like a couple of children. Jack, being the nimblest of them all, scooted through the propped open door quickest, before sliding across the wood floor to the spot where they'd performed their Weezer tribute. A box labelled, "The Three" awaited them.

Jack handed it to Melody, suggesting this was her clue to open, because this game had all been about her. She sat in the middle of the floor and opened the box. Tanner and Jack stood over her, watching. Melody pulled out the note and read it aloud.

Melody, Jack, and Tanner,

It means so much that you trusted me enough to take part in this little hunt. It may seem juvenile, and an immature way to apologize to a group of adults, but to be honest, being here at Sweet Clover brings out the preteen girl in me—in the best way—and it seemed like the right thing to do.

I hope you will accept my multiple apologies and can find it in your hearts to forgive me. I have spent years working on myself, and I'm sure you all have grown and changed as well, but I still feel we are all meant to be friends. That summer enmeshed our lives, mainly connecting the four of you throughout the years. I will have some catching up to do, but I would love the opportunity.

Piper

She signed the note with her name and at the bottom left a quote from one of Melody's favourite songs, "Iris". Melody quietly sang the rest of the chorus aloud.

She wasn't a singer by any stretch of the imagination, however, compared to the raspy tone of John Rzeznik, she sounded soft and sweet. Tanner stood with his hands in his pockets, looking around the room awkwardly. When Melody finished, she looked up to see Jack's eyes were glassy before he looked in the other direction to hide the evidence. It wasn't his style to be so forthright with his emotions, so it didn't surprise her that he wanted to keep them tucked away.

Jack reached his hand down to pull Melody up from the floor. For a moment, they locked eyes, and years of unspoken sentiments passed silently between them. Melody gave her telltale shy smile, and with a quick squeeze, she dropped Jack's hand. The two of them turned to face Tanner, who had witnessed the entire scene, though seemed to be oblivious to the depth of it.

"So, what do we do about the note?" he asked, to cut the tension.

"After all this time, all this effort, all the sincerity Piper poured out between these pages, I can't imagine not forgiving her and seeing how our lives can all move on together. Besides, I have things to apologize for too," Melody concluded.

"I agree. There is so much that can change and shape a friendship over the years, and while this one had a rough start, it's important to see where it goes from here, especially for the two of you," Jack agreed.

"I'm worried about Cody, honestly. I reserve my vote until we've spoken to him," Tanner said.

They all exchanged glances.

"Shit, did we ditch him?" Jack asked through a laugh.

"Oops. We should probably go find him," Melody replied.

"Let's go!" Tanner shouted and seemingly knowing exactly which direction to head in, ran out the door, sprinting across the centre of camp and up the bunkie porch.

"Where are you going?" Melody called after him.

"Well, if they've fallen back in love, they're probably in her room unable to keep their hands off each other!" Tanner laughed and pulled open the door.

"And if they haven't?" Jack called out.

"Then I know exactly where Cody will be..." Tanner trailed off as he ran up the stairs two by two.

He pounded on Piper's bedroom door and waited to hear a sound. There was nothing. He knocked again, this time a little more gently, and waited, but still nothing. Tanner turned around and headed back down the stairs, his face crumpled.

"They're not there," he said, disheartened.

"Well, that doesn't mean they haven't worked things out," Melody said.

"They might still be in the throes of their reunion wherever Cody's last clue led to," Jack suggested with hope.

Melody glanced at her watch. "It's already after five. The dinner bell is going to ring soon and they'll come down to eat, from wherever they are. Let's wait on the porch."

The three friends shuffled back out the door and spotted Cody and Piper sitting on the dining hall porch, where they'd just come from moments earlier. Cody beamed from ear to ear, and Piper leaned into him in a way that could only mean one thing.

The five met between the porches like a stand-off turned friendly. Piper moved to hug Melody, and Melody accepted and reciprocated.

"I am so grateful you all followed my clues. I'm so sorry about everything. Can we start over?"

Melody stayed quiet for a minute, processing everything that had transpired between them, until it all clicked into place.

"Piper, you spent all afternoon apologizing in your notes, but none of this was ever your fault. We didn't understand it then, but we do now. You were sick, and we did what we thought was best to get you help, but then we disappeared. No follow-through. You didn't deserve that. You deserved friends who were checking in and making sure you were okay. We are the ones who should be sorry, and we are."

Jack and Tanner nodded in agreement.

"I understand you wanted some resolution, and I'm not sure if this was what you were expecting, but I am so grateful. You need to understand how happy I am to be alive. How magical it is to be back at Sweet Clover. None of that could have happened without all of you getting me back to the hospital. It's like I'm getting a second chance, like this can be a complete do-over of the last decade of my life. Almost like I'm a twelve-year-old camper again," Piper explained.

Tanner looked at Cody. "What do you have to say, Code?"

"Everything feels like the movies," he said through a smile.

Melody, Tanner, and Jack all started laughing, remembering the song from just moments earlier.

"What's so funny?" Cody asked.

"You had to be there," Jack said.

"Inside joke," Tanner said at the same time.

"You brought this entire day full circle without even knowing," Melody added.

"So, we're good?" Piper asked.

"We're friends, Piper, and friends take the good times with the bad. It might take a bit to get back on track, with all the history between us, but I know we can figure it out!" Melody said.

The dinner bell cut through the conversation right on cue, and people poured into the centre of camp from their various cabins.

***

The five friends enjoyed a hot camp dinner together, something they didn't know they'd been missing after complaining about the camp food over the years. During the meal, staff and volunteers from years past milled around the dining hall, saying hello to old friends, exchanging long hugs. It was quite a sight to see. Before dessert, the director, Leslie, stepped up to the front of the room to make an announcement. She waited until the room fell silent, and eagerly clasped her hands in front of her and looked around.

"Seeing this room full of volunteers and staff from the last two decades of Camp Sweet Clover summers makes my heart so full. When I took over the camp in the early '80s, I had no idea how much it would grow and change over the years. I have loved the journey; it has brought me closer to nature, provided me with lifelong relationships to cherish, taught me how to be the person others need without losing myself, and it has been nothing short of life-changing. But this, bringing back all of you for a weekend together, this must be my favourite moment to date. I plan to make it a yearly tradition, and I hope you will all join us again next year. We still have an entire weekend of fun ahead though, so let's not worry about the future too much. I hope you will all come by the office and have a coffee with me—yes, I still run on coffee and compliments—but otherwise you are free to do what you wish! We will follow the normal camp schedule, but you, being adults, are not bound to it. Come and go as you please. This is your camp experience. I want you to enjoy every minute. We will have a wide game after dinner, and the bell for campfire is at seven o'clock. I hope to see you all there. Now please go back to enjoying this delicious meal!"

The room exploded with cheers and clapping as Leslie wandered back to her table. Melody's heart about burst with happiness. She was getting a do-over of her camp experience and reliving the days when Sweet Clover subsisted as her second home. She was thrilled she was getting to spend the weekend with the four people surrounding her at the table.

"Can you pass the bread, please?" Tanner nudged Melody out of her daydream.

"Oh, sorry," she said, flashing a smile, and passed the platter of garlic rolls.

Jack looked at her across the table and smirked, and Cody stared at Piper across from him too. Melody wondered if this could be the start of the rest of their lives. Would they all be together forever? After everything they'd been through, it seemed too good to be true.

The group finished their dinner and went their separate ways to get changed and ready for the game. Melody and Piper hadn't been joiners when they were campers or volunteers, but now taking part in the wide game seemed like the most enjoyable thing they could do right now.

Melody called after Piper as she walked up the bunkie porch steps, "Why don't you bring your stuff to Marigolds?"

Piper turned to look at the guys, and they all nodded.

"Okay!" she exclaimed and ran into the building and up the stairs.

Piper arrived at the cabin ten minutes later, changed and carrying her suitcase.

"Hey, those two bunks are free over there. Unfortunately for you, TJ claimed the counsellor beds, so you'll have a tight squeeze if you were planning to bunk with Cody," Melody said with a giggle.

"TJ?" Piper questioned.

"Oh, yes, that's what I have called Tanner and Jack since they became a couple," Melody explained.

"I always wondered if you two would end up together. I love that for you both! And I'm not picky about the beds. I'm just so happy to be here with you all. It was pretty lonely up in the loft, especially with all my history there," Piper said.

"Wait, back up. You knew we loved each other before we did?" Tanner asked.

Piper just smirked.

Cody was lost in his own world, smiling at nothing. Melody had never seen him so happy, though she still had concerns about how this would all pan out once they left camp on Monday. She guessed that was future-Cody's problem though, and for now she should just enjoy their happiness.

Piper got her bunk ready and sat down beside Cody on the bed next to hers. "This is it," Melody overheard Piper whisper.

"This is it," he repeated and kissed her on the cheek. But forever being interrupted, the bell rang for wide game.

"Let's go!" Tanner shouted and flung open the cabin door.

The group filed out of the cabin and down the stairs and made their way to the lower field to find out what their game would be for the evening. They should have guessed, though; capture the flag, a camp classic. It was a great way to meet people you're unfamiliar with, so it was often a "first night of camp" choice. Leslie split the group into two teams based on their cabins and handed out the flags.

"On your mark, get set, go!" she yelled, and everyone

scattered impressively quick for a bunch of adults playing a children's game. *This will be a good fight. A win is what we all need to cement this perfect this day.*

Capture the flag was over before it began. People were getting tired or injured right out of the gates, as is the problem with young adults—most of whom have been sitting writing essays for the last few years—playing a game made for energetic kids. Everyone seemed to have a great time though, and laughter rang throughout the camp. Melody noticed, however, that everyone seemed relieved when the bell rang to end the game and to signal people to get ready for the campfire. Leslie didn't crown a winner, but no one seemed to mind.

This pre-campfire process, like always, included changing into mosquito-survival clothing like pants and long sleeved-shirts, and dousing each other in bug spray, before heading back toward the dining hall. The kitchen had prepared Melody's favourite treat, haystacks, for a snack before the campfire. She truly was getting an authentic camp experience as a 21-year-old woman.

The friends had mostly stuck together through the game, although Cody and Piper disappeared for a bit in the middle, *shocking*. They all left for campfire together too. Jack and Tanner lead the pack, holding hands and skipping down the path. Melody walked in the middle, envious of their love, but happy for them all the same. Cody and Piper brought up the rear, not holding hands, but doing that cutesy shoulder to shoulder walk people do when they can't stand to be six inches away from each other.

Melody contemplated her life back home. Everything had been going according to plan. She was doing well at school, despite how all-consuming it was, and she had Riley. She wasn't ready for the next step, even if he decided they were, but she also couldn't bring herself to end it. That was something she needed to sort out, sooner than later, and she promised herself she would make a decision before she returned home. It wasn't fair to Riley.

The friends arrived at campfire and picked a bench at the back, where the troublemakers sat. Leslie and a few of the other staff were at the front with their guitars ready to get things started, but it always took way longer than necessary to get everyone in their spots and quiet. Leslie cleared her throat. Melody remembered how annoying it had been in her camper days, when they were always getting reprimanded. *Not much has changed.*

The campfire delivered the perfect amount of nostalgia Melody had been looking for. They sang all her favourites and even took requests. Of course she asked for "If I Had a Boat". Piper's clue had brought the song back to her mind, and now it was stuck in her head and she needed to sing it out. When the staff started strumming, the friends all clasped hands and started belting out the words. Melody remembered how funny it had seemed as a camper to shout "kiss my ass" in the middle of the song, so she sang it extra loud just because she could.

Melody fully embraced each moment of the weekend. She had been wishing to be back at CSC for so long, and now she was, so she did her best to appreciate every part. As they all crawled into bed that night, there was a lot of quiet chatter between the two couples. Melody may have been a little left out, but she turned on her flashlight and journaled instead of resigning herself to sadness over it. She had planned to write every night so she wouldn't forget a single second.

She hoped they would keep coming every year to keep reliving her glory days at Camp Sweet Clover, however, once there were more careers and eventually kids involved, she knew it may get a little more difficult. Melody sighed. The idea broke her heart a little, but she crossed her fingers they would make it a tradition, because she would have to battle some serious post-camp blues when they left on Monday. This was still her favourite place in the world, and now, after reconciling with Piper and moving through all her feelings about the summer of 1994, it embodied that more strongly.

At school, Melody learned how easy it was to become attached to places where you had monumental shifts in your life, in your personality, or mental wellness. That was probably what had happened here, most 20-somethings weren't still obsessed with their childhood summer camp, but it didn't bother her one bit. The smell of the Sweet Clover air was everything. Unfortunately, Melody was all too aware that the second they pulled off the dirt road at the end of the weekend, it would all be a distant memory. No photograph would freeze time and keep the sights and smells fresh in her mind. No amount of trying could hold on to the weight of Jack's hand in hers. It was already slipping away.

CHAPTER 31
AUGUST 2000
PIPER

Piper woke up on Saturday morning, ready to conquer the world. She had acknowledged her past mistakes and her friends had forgiven her. She and Cody were back together, or at least, somewhat unofficially, they were seeing each other. Everything seemed to have worked out in her favour, and that wasn't something she was used to.

She laid in bed, listening to the sounds of everyone sleeping. Major snoring came from Tanner and Jack's bed, although she couldn't tell who it was, silence from Cody beside her, and the tossing and turning of Melody about to wake up in her bunk.

They would all be awake soon, so Piper wanted to take advantage of being alone to get some writing done. She slipped out of bed and threw a hoodie on over her pyjamas, slid into her Birks at the door, and crept out and down the stairs. She wandered over to Morningview Shores and sat down with her journal. Piper detailed all the events of the day before as the sun rose over the lake, and it ended up almost four pages long. Sticking to her routines was important for her mental health, so she allowed herself all the time she needed. When the bell rang for breakfast, she finished penning her entry and walked back up to the cabin.

The bell had woken her friends. Melody, dressed and ready, sat in bed, writing, just as Piper had moments before. The girls really were more alike than they ever thought possible.

The guys were crawling out of bed and scrambling to get warm clothes on to make it to the dining hall before the other cabins. If you were last to arrive, you had to lead grace, and no one in their group, aside from Jack maybe, wanted to be doing that at not-yet eight o'clock. Thankfully, they arrived early compared to the other groups, and Piper wondered how many of them had forgotten the rule.

After a nostalgic run through of Johnny Appleseed, everyone sauntered inside to find a camp-favourite prepared and steaming on their tables—baked oatmeal.

Piper watched Melody lean into Jack and say, "I'm pretty sure they planned this entire weekend for me!" Jack chuckled and nodded.

The table ate silently for the rest of breakfast, too busy shovelling the maple syrup covered loaf into their mouths for chatter. Leslie arrived at the front of the room again to offer a brief insight into their day.

"Good morning, friends! I hope you had a wonderful sleep last night! We will get started after breakfast with the first session. All your favourite camp activities are open except for the waterfront. It's too dang cold in the morning for swimming, so those activities will be open for the afternoon sessions. Don't forget to be safe and please leave your activity areas the way you found them! Have fun!"

The dining hall filled with the sound of murmuring voices as everyone discussed which activities they wanted to do. Piper had plans to head to arts and crafts—old habits die hard. But Cody set his heart on archery. Melody offered to accompany Piper, and

Tanner and Jack chose the climbing wall where, if they were being honest, they would likely stay all morning.

Everyone dispersed to their various activities after breakfast, and Piper was authentically herself with Melody, probably for the first time. As she sat down with some embroidery thread, she wondered if Melody was as enthusiastic about their progress as she was. Instead of exhausting herself wondering, she decided just to ask.

"I'm glad we're doing this," Piper said.

"Crafting?" Melody asked with a laugh.

"No," Piper said. "Spending some time just the two of us. I know we decided we'd work it out yesterday, but I would still like to solidify our relationship and get started in the right direction before we all go home. I don't want us to all go back to the way things were when we leave here."

"I get that, and agree. There isn't really any way things can go back to the way they were, though. I mean, I feel like this is a fresh start for us all, and we have this incredible weekend to spend time together. We're all stuck being friends now. Wait, are you making friendship bracelets?" Melody asked, trying to keep a straight face.

"Uh…" Piper said.

Melody threw her hand to her mouth to cover her laughter, but Piper was smirking.

"Might as well embrace the full camp experience!" Melody said as she grabbed a handful of thread.

After finishing their bracelets, they tied them on each other's wrists, and left the art cabin to look for the guys. They found Jack and Tanner in the lower field, both halfway up a climbing wall, and Melody sat down to watch them.

Piper continued walking to the north field where the archery targets were, hoping to find Cody. She found him lying in the field in the sun with his eyes closed.

"Cody?" Piper whispered.

Cody twitched from the surprise then opened his eyes, shielding them with his hand so he could see her, and his face lit up. "Hey," he said.

"Whatcha doing?" she asked.

"Oh, my arm tired out pretty fast, so here I am, enjoying the sun and the Sweet Clover air."

"Everyone has mentioned the air this weekend. It's just magical, isn't it? I had kind of forgotten. Or maybe we don't really notice as kids?" Piper wondered aloud as she lay down beside him.

The late-summer sun on their skin was rejuvenating, and they laid there for the rest of the session. Piper struggled to remember a time when she felt this happy, and she hoped it would last. The moment didn't, however, as the bell for the second session rang, and the pair sat up in unison. Cody leaned over and gave Piper a kiss on the cheek. She grinned and pulled him up with her as she stood.

"Where are we headed?" Cody asked.

"Anywhere you want," Piper said, and led him by the hand across the field.

***

The five friends had an incredible weekend together, enjoying every minute of camp life. They swam, canoed, laughed, ate way too much, sang songs at campfire, and even took part in each night's wide game. They talked about the future and the past, and they spent the entire time as a group, except for the handful of times that Piper and Cody snuck off to make out like teenagers.

Monday morning came far too quickly, and there was a lot of discussion about when they would see each other next. Melody promised to bring Riley to TJ's house to meet everyone, and Piper assured Melody that she would call her weekly to check in. Their friendship was finally blossoming the way Piper secretly hoped it would back when they were young girls, despite all the walls she put up in their first few interactions. There had been a lot of life and loss that had transpired since that summer, but they were working through it and growing closer by the day. Piper and Melody both expressed how sad they were to leave, although the guys, Jack and Tanner at least, seemed more eager to get home.

The hardest part came when Piper needed to say goodbye to Cody. They had decided the night before to be something, officially. They weren't sure what it would take to navigate the distance, but they were determined to find out if they could make it work. There was plenty of pouting as they packed up the cabin, and again as they loaded their bags into their cars, which continued for almost an hour while they chatted to prolong their goodbye in the parking lot.

Arriving at Sweet Clover, Piper was in the dark about what the weekend would bring her. She waffled between excitement and terror, and early on couldn't decide if everything she'd done had been a mistake. She recalled her panic attack, which seemed like ages ago now, and how she had considered leaving before they saw each other. Instead, everything had gone almost perfectly, and she was over the moon. She decided that this was the good karma coming to her from her years of traumatic upbringing and all the work she'd put in to heal herself, and the help she offered other women to do the same at work.

In that moment, Piper realized how much she missed the Rose residents and her job. It made her wonder how she would ever leave it, but if she needed to do that to be with Cody, she would. Those couple of days with him had lit her heart on fire, and she wanted to do everything possible to make their lives together long and happy.

Before Cody got into the car, Piper grabbed his hand and

looked him in the eyes and said, "I love you," before she turned and walked away without waiting for a reply.

It might be premature, with them only having been back on speaking terms for three days, but they had been together before, and they hadn't lost that love for each other after all their years apart. *There is something here worth seeing through.*

CHAPTER 32

SEPTEMBER 2000

MELODY

The friends all returned home to their various lives across the province and kept in touch through letters and phone calls. Piper wrote to Melody often.

> September 17, 2000
>
> Melody,
>
> How are you doing? What is new at home? How is Riley? Things are going well here. Cody and I talk every night. We're doing a great job of keeping our relationship alive despite the distance. I am having a bit of a tough time being here alone, though, and I am so restless at work.
>
> I have a million ideas of how to help my residents, but there are no funds to work with. It's a common problem in the non-profit sector,

of course, and I know I'm not alone in my frustration. I've spent so much time researching ways to get funding for the shelter and I keep hitting wall after wall! I hope one day I'll be able to run an organization where funding isn't a problem, though I'm sure that's much easier said than done.

Tell me more about your school. I'd love to hear how you like it and what you're learning. I hope we can see each other again soon!

Piper

The girls continued to grow their friendship through letters and over the phone throughout the autumn. Melody had returned to school for her fourth year of psychology, and although she loved it, her workload overwhelmed her, keeping her constantly busy. After everything that happened at Sweet Clover, Melody felt she had worked through a lot of her trauma, and with the help of her therapist, she was well on her way to mental wellness for the first time in years.

Of course, she knew mental health was ever-fluctuating, but she was more stable than she had been since she was fifteen. Now, she easily grasped all the tricky intricacies of her studies without having her judgement clouded by her own traumas.

Jack also wrote to Melody often. He and Tanner loved their new life living together and were planning out their next few years. In his letters now, Jack always gave play-by-play updates of their life—it seemed like he no longer compartmentalized as much. Melody loved getting to know him better through his correspondence. He also burned her CDs she needed to hear and talked about plans for the next time they could see each other.

She of course, replied to each one quickly. It wasn't an easy way to maintain the unique type of bond they shared, but she loved it for that reason.

The group planned to get together during Melody's school break in October, and she would introduce Riley to everyone at long last. To say she was terrified would be an understatement.

> October 3, 2000
>
> Piper,
>
> I am so excited for us all to get together this month! Though, I'd be lying if I said I wasn't nervous. I know everyone will like Riley because I like Riley, but that's not really what I'm nervous about.
>
> I'm sure you can tell that my relationship with Jack is a little outside of a normal friendship, and Riley understands that. But if you haven't ever had that kind of connection, can you really understand or even prepare yourself for what that might look like?
>
> If you want to know the truth, I almost broke up with him when I got home from the reunion. I think it was a bit of a wake-up call for me, seeing how in love both TJ and you and Cody are, and that Riley and I don't have that, even after a year and a half together.
>
> Maybe I'm just putting too much pressure on us when our lives are so hectic? My head is in another place so much of the time. But maybe my heart is too?
>
> Help.
>
> Melody

Melody didn't receive another letter from Piper before the weekend arrived. She could have called to get advice, but despite her plea for guidance, it wasn't really something Piper could help her with.

It didn't help when Riley told Melody that he anticipated being the sixth wheel in their group.

"You guys have been knit together by a single moment years ago. Plus a few long breaks, impossible to understand connections, a place I've never been, and a reunion I wasn't a part of."

"I understand. It must be intimidating to slip into a well-established group like ours, but I assure you, these are some of the most welcoming people you'll ever meet. New people come to camp every summer and assimilate into friend groups that last a lifetime," Melody reassured him.

"Melody, this isn't camp."

"Well, you know what I mean."

When Melody expected an affirming response, Riley simply looked away, alluding that he did not, in fact, know what she meant.

Jack and Tanner had offered to host that year, so everyone travelled to Orillia for the weekend. Melody planned to arrive a bit later so that the other friends could all settle in before she and Riley joined them. As she rang the doorbell at TJ's, her excitement over seeing her friends was strong, but not enough to quell the worry behind all her thoughts about Riley.

Jack answered the door and scooped her up in a hug without even saying a word. He put her back on her feet and playfully pushed her away from him to pull Riley in for a hug too. Riley's eyes grew wide, surprised by the friendly greeting. Evidently, Melody didn't do a good job of preparing him, but it was a good icebreaker. Jack laughed as he saw the startled look on Riley's face when he let him go and ushered the two of them into the house.

"I'm so glad you're here!" Jack said, pulling Melody by the hand. "Everyone is here already. Hey everyone, meet Riley!" he shouted as they rounded the corner into the living room.

Everyone waved and said hello and they got right to the business of grilling Riley, before he'd even sat down.

"So, what are you studying?" Tanner asked.

"Psych, like Melody. That's how we met."

"Where did you grow up?" Jack asked without giving Riley a moment to breathe.

"In Vancouver. I travelled to Ontario for a trip during high school and decided I wanted to come back to attend university."

The questions persisted until timers started going off in the kitchen. Jack was putting his culinary skills on full display, and had to tend to multiple dishes.

Riley disappeared into the kitchen under the guise of offering to help with the food. Melody, still a nosey human after all these years, albeit a much more empathetic one, wanted in on their conversation. She rose from her seat and wandered around the room, pretending to admire TJ's new house, and lingered by the kitchen doorway, just out of sight.

"Jack," Riley said, "I wanted to ask you something."

"Sure, what's up?" Jack returned.

"Well, you are one of the most important people in Melody's life, and it's obvious that you guys have some sort of special relationship that no one else comes between. That's perfectly fine with me. I love that she has you. The connection between you two is something I'm unfamiliar with, but I felt you deserved this courtesy..." he trailed off. He sounded nervous, but no one could have been more on edge than Melody in that moment.

"I would like to ask Melody to move in with me, but she is

such a closed book. I can't even figure out if she wants that. Do you have any advice? She hasn't even said 'I love you' yet."

Silence. For a moment or two, the shock must have rendered Jack speechless, but he recovered and shifted his focus to answer Riley's question.

"I don't know you all that well, man, but I can read Melody like the back of my hand. I don't want to rain on your parade, but if she was ready for a big step like that, you wouldn't have to wonder."

Melody heard Riley sigh and felt her heart breaking. Not only was moving in together a nail in the coffin for everything she'd ever held in her heart for Jack, but she couldn't imagine being anywhere near ready for that type of commitment.

Like Riley mentioned, she hadn't even said those three magic words every relationship needs expressed before a giant leap like that. She'd always finagled her way around saying them, and Riley never seemed to notice. *I guess he did, though? Perhaps he expected a grand gesture would hurry me along?*

Jack busied himself with dishes again, and Riley changed the subject to something about Jack's house. Melody took this as her queue to leave and sauntered away before the two might leave the kitchen and catch her in the act. Her heart threatened to escape her chest with the force of its beats—not with happiness or excitement, but with guilt and dread.

Jack and Riley emerged a few moments later, and when Melody saw the unhappy look on Riley's face, she felt bad for eavesdropping. She couldn't stew in her emotions long though, because the entire group was in for a surprise just moments later.

"Okay!" Piper said, a little too excited, "now that we're all here, Cody and I have an announcement to make—"

"We're getting married!" Cody interrupted as Piper shoved her hand out for them all to examine her ring. Melody glanced at Riley and saw his eyes widen and his face grimace before he pulled himself together.

With cheers, congratulations, hugs, and questions about the wedding, Melody felt immense relief for the distraction.

"It's fast by traditional standards, but, like, is it really? We both were thinking about each other the entire time we were apart! It doesn't seem fast to us. It feels like it was a foregone conclusion the moment we got back together," Piper explained.

"Yup, I was looking at rings like two weeks after getting home from camp," Cody said with a sheepish grin. "However, we want to keep everything under wraps for now. The details are going to be a surprise."

The group filled the rest of the evening with delicious food, great conversation, a few competitive squabbles about board games, a quaint autumn bonfire, and tons of laughter. From the outside, you never could have imagined what these friends had been through together, or who the newbie was. Riley slid right in like he'd been there through it all.

Everyone retired to their various beds late into the night, until only Jack and Melody remained. They sat in front of the fire, enjoying the quiet comfort that always came with the two of them, alone together, neither needing to fill the silence. Jack picked up his guitar and started plucking.

He started to sing. He sang about a girl who should be among the wildflowers, a girl who should be somewhere she felt free. He sang about her finding a lover, and how much she deserved those things.

Melody continued without missing a beat. She sang about following her heart. She sang about having a home. She sang about being far away from her trouble and worries.

Jacked plucked the last few bars and let them fade out into the night air. He put his guitar on the seat next to him and stood, avoiding any display of emotion. *Typical.* He turned toward Melody and got close enough to give her a quick kiss on the forehead, then mumbled, "Goodnight, kid," before he turned and walked off towards the house where his partner slept.

Melody sat in silence as a few rogue tears slid down her cheeks. Her heart was both full of love and tearing apart at once. When she was a little girl, she believed everyone had one soulmate, and that soulmate would be your one true love, and you'd find each other and get married and live happily ever after.

Now that couldn't be farther from the truth. She no longer believed there was only one soulmate for everyone, as it had become clear to her that sometimes soulmates weren't even the person you spend your life with. There were different types of soulmates too—best friend soulmates and lover soulmates.

It had taken her years to distinguish between the two, and even then, she would still sometimes get it twisted for a moment.

Melody sat in front of the fire until her tears dried and then finally took herself to bed, where a dream of wildflowers awaited her.

From October to February, Melody spent hours on the phone with Piper, listening to her brainstorm almost every detail about the wedding. Melody still didn't know where it was taking place. Piper and Cody had originally planned an extended engagement, because it was so soon after getting together, but at the start of the new year, something changed their plans.

It was still unbelievable to Melody that she had friends who were getting married. Wasn't she just a camper a few years ago? It made sense, though, for them. Piper had no family to speak of, and she wanted—needed—an official one, and Cody's Christian parents wouldn't let them live together until they were married, so there was pressure from his side too.

School assignments and late-night phone calls with Piper took up a lot of Melody's time, but since returning from TJ's, she had also been trying to make up for her carelessness with Riley's feelings. The weekend with her camp friends made her realize while the other couples were head over heels for each other; their relationships were also hard work. Especially Piper and Cody's, which existed only on the phone most of the time. If Melody wanted that kind of love in her life, she knew it wasn't going to just happen. She had to put in the effort too.

While there had been little progress on her end in terms of longterm commitment, she could tell from Riley's mood he was feeling more content with the situation. Melody hoped eventually she would let her walls down with Riley and they could move forward, but she would just have to wait and see.

After stalking her mail carrier for days, knowing it was on its way, Piper and Cody's wedding invite arrived during the bleakest week of Ontarian winter. The world had been endlessly grey for months, and Melody's patience for spring's return was hanging on by a thread. She almost screamed when she finally saw the envelope in her mailbox, offering a small ray of sunlight to bring joy and excitement to Melody's life. On the outside, it looked like a casual outdoor-style wedding invite—a trend that had become popular in the last few years as even religious folks shied away from church ceremonies in favour of something more modern. On the inside, however, the contents blew Melody's mind.

CODY MICHA HUGHES &
PIPER JULIE SHEPARD
INVITE YOU TO SHARE IN THEIR JOY
AT THEIR UPCOMING WEDDING
SATURDAY, JUNE 3, 2001
AT 4:30 IN THE AFTERNOON
AT CAMP SWEET CLOVER, ONTARIO

Melody picked up the phone and dialled Piper.

"You. are. not!" she squealed into the receiver.

Piper laughed. "We are! Are you excited about going back?"

"Yes! I can't wait! I'm putting a countdown in my agenda right now as we speak!"

Melody worked her butt off all the way through her countdown, trying to finish up her psychology degree. When she reached the end of April and handed in her last exam, Melody barely even thought about graduation, and immediately switched to preparations for the wedding, and how great it would be to be back at Camp Sweet Clover so soon.

She spent days scouring the malls for the perfect dress to wear, and of course, had to consult TJ too before deciding on the right one. She picked a lacy yellow sundress, and opted to attend barefoot, because besides Birkenstocks, nothing said camp like your feet in the dirt. At home she only ever wore Converse, for any occasion no matter the formality, but camp was different.

"Bare feet?" Riley questioned her choice, never having been to a wedding, or to camp, let alone to the two intertwined.

"Absolutely," Melody said with confidence.

"And what should I wear?"

"Khakis with your Birks would be perfect," Melody suggested.

"Okay, if you're sure," Riley agreed, despite being much less confident than Melody in the choice.

CHAPTER 34
JUNE 2001
MELODY

Luckily for Melody, with just a few weeks between the chaos of final exams and the wedding, the time passed quickly, and she was driving back to Camp Sweet Clover once again.

Close friends and family arrived Friday night, and each group had their own cabin, just like their reunion weekend. Melody spent Friday afternoon showing Riley around, explaining all the different areas of camp, and cluing him in to where all the memories she always talked about happened. The lake was frigid the first weekend in June, but they sat on the dock and dipped their toes in, watching the sunset over the trees.

"It is beautiful here, I can see why you love it so much," Riley said.

"It is, though more than the beauty, it's all the emotions that are wrapped up in this place. When I'm here, it's like I'm home," Melody explained.

"I can see how you would feel that way. That must make it difficult to be anywhere else, though."

"You know, I've never really made that connection. I guess I've been having to exist in a place every day that doesn't feel like home. Maybe that's why I have such a hard time planning for the future."

The sun dipped behind the horizon far too quickly, and the pair could no longer bear their frozen toes, so they returned to the cabin. Unsurprisingly, they found TJ, Cody, and Piper knee deep in a board game that covered the cabin floor. Melody laughed at the familiarity of the scene, as she and Riley sat down to watch the game unfold.

Despite the Carcassonne pieces spread all over, the game moved quickly, and it wasn't long before Jack had come out victorious, as he often did. He offered another round to the friends, but they all shook their heads, citing various levels of fatigue. Cody and Piper retired to their private cabin, one of the senior boys' homes, named after a tree that Melody couldn't remember, deep in the woods for their privacy.

Saturday morning came and went, and the camp was bustling with people preparing for the evening's festivities. Melody helped Piper's work-friends set up the dining hall with the decorations and place settings for dinner after the ceremony. TJ and Riley turned the Fraser Bunkie into a dance hall for the reception. They added decorations, set up a high-tech sound system, and prepared the drink bar. The camp didn't let alcohol on the premises, but they made an exception for the wedding with a promise that everyone would be on their best behaviour.

Satisfied with her work in the dining hall, Melody hustled down to the ceremony location—the dock, of course—to ensure they had everything ready there too. There were chairs lining the staggered terraces down to the beach, and flowers along the dock. The view was spectacular, and the ceremony would turn out perfectly. Her next stop was hair and makeup, where Piper had already been for hours, entrusting the preparation of her special day to her very best friends.

Melody walked into the cabin and Piper took her breath away. The hairstylist had pulled Piper's hair back from her face in a half-up configuration, with the ends braided together, and the rest falling in curled tendrils down her back. She had simple, barely there, makeup, which accentuated the natural good looks she'd grown into over the years. Someone also painted her toenails and fingernails as she sat still, afraid to smudge or flatten or ruin anything.

"You look incredible," Melody said in awe.

"Thank you!" Piper blushed. "I haven't had anything like this done before. It is wild! But I'm almost done here and then it'll be your turn, maid of honour!"

Melody just blinked at her. She had assumed one of Piper's work-friends would be the maid of honour and was completely taken-aback.

"So, I didn't officially ask you," Piper started, "but I didn't want you to bear the pressure of extra responsibilities while trying to finish your school year. I assumed you would help when needed, because that's just who you are, and I was sure you would be here for me through all the excitement of the day. Anyway, I guess now that most of the work is done, I'm asking."

"Yes, of course I'll be your maid of honour, but I don't have a speech prepared!" Melody said, panicking.

"Oh, don't worry about that, if you just thank everyone for coming, that will be perfect," Piper assured her.

Of course, Melody wouldn't just thank everyone for coming, but that took the pressure off a bit. Piper climbed out of her chair and motioned for Melody to sit for her hair and makeup. Her brain ran a mile a minute as she tried to piece a speech together on a whim.

"What about my dress?" Melody asked.

"I spoke to Jack a few weeks back. He told me what colour you are wearing, and I planned your bouquet around it. Don't worry, you will look great," Piper said.

"And you're okay with me being barefoot? Because I literally didn't bring shoes."

"Girl, I'll have bare feet under my wedding dress. I wouldn't have it any other way," Piper replied with a grin.

Okay then. Now I just need a speech. Melody picked her brain for any memories of wedding speeches in movies and tv shows. Deciding to gather more intel, she threw questions at Piper like a journalist.

"Did you write your own vows?"

"Of course!" Piper replied.

"How did you choose Tanner to walk you down the aisle?"

"I don't have that many reliable men in my life... and he promised not to let me trip." Piper smiled.

"He'll be a great escort! Do you have much family coming?" Melody inquired, wording her question cautiously as Piper had little family to begin with.

"My mom didn't reply to the invite, though I'm not surprised because we haven't talked in years. My grandma, who you know I reconnected with after the reunion, didn't want to travel this far, but sent her best wishes."

"Well, you have lots of friends to celebrate with!" Melody said. "Oh, and I brought you this. I'm not sure if you want to put it in your bouquet or something, but it felt right."

Melody handed Piper a hand-stitched badge, with a green clover in the middle, and the letters CSC on it. "You're getting married today! I think there should be a badge for that!"

"Oh, Melody, it's perfect! Thank you!" Piper said, her voice wavering with emotion as she traced her fingers along the stitching.

Melody was still racking her brain for the right words for her maid of honour speech when it came time to go to the ceremony. She was ready otherwise, wearing her sundress and bare feet. The stylist had perfected her hair and makeup, creating a reflection she'd never seen before; one she couldn't decide if she liked. What she looked like wasn't important though, today was about Piper.

Melody zipped Piper into her floor length white, boho style lace dress. The choice was miles ahead of the current fashion trends but would look beautiful while admiring wedding photos 20-years down the road when it inevitably would come back in style.

"When Cody got approval to host our wedding here, I was positive that I wanted a dress that complimented the natural environment and the wild and free atmosphere of summer camp," Piper explained.

"This dress, paired with your elegant hippy hair and bare feet, does just that. You look like a 1970s goddess!" Melody said, and Piper laughed.

As the women walked down the hill and across the centre of camp towards the waterfront, they both became visibly nervous. Tanner had promised to keep Piper upright while travelling down the steps, but what about Melody? She had to walk them on her own. They both giggled nervously as they got closer. Piper stayed tucked down the pathway while Melody made her way to the top of the steps. Tanner stood, looking so handsome in his grey suit, waiting for the bride. He gave Melody a smile and a nod. She took a deep breath and continued her walk.

She hadn't even hit the second step before she started thanking her intuition for wearing a short dress and bare feet. Those choices saved her while descending the steep terraces. When she reached the bottom, the music changed, and the familiar strumming of Cody's acoustic version of "Follow You Down" by the Gin Blossoms played. Piper appeared at the top, and Tanner slid his bent arm through hers and whispered something in her ear before he led her down the stairs.

Tanner and Piper walked slowly to both prevent an embarrassing fall, and to line their arrival up with the end of the song. They'd practiced about fifteen times the night before and were both confident they would nail the timing.

All eyes were on the beautiful bride. Some older attendees seemed confused with the unconventional song choice, however, Melody understood it wasn't a choice; it had been the only option after everything Cody and Piper had been through.

Melody watched as Piper didn't look at Cody all the way down, presumably because his expression would make her cry and ruin her makeup. Piper had confided in Melody earlier that the last thing she wanted to do was be a blubbering mess through the ceremony.

Tanner and Piper arrived at the bottom and walked along the dock, stopping in perfect timing. He kissed Piper on the cheek and gave her hand to Cody as the last words of the song came through the speaker. Cody's face flushed, either with the mid-afternoon heat and his cumbersome suit, or perhaps his embarrassment at being at the centre of attention, something he'd hated so much that he'd retired from his potential college sports career in favour of being a nobody in the hallways and working in retail. Melody wasn't supposed to know that part, but Piper didn't have any secrets from her anymore.

A soft breeze made the foliage dance along the dock, filling the air with the early summer fragrance of wildflowers. Melody closed her eyes and breathed in, wanting to remember every moment of this day. Piper blinked furiously. *She must be trying to hold back tears threatening the edges of her eyes.* Cody smiled at her, and the officiant began.

The ceremony continued without a hitch. Their vows were stunningly beautiful, and Melody wondered how such quiet elegance emerged from these two chaotic friends of hers.

"Piper Julie Shepard. You are and will forever be the most beautiful girl in the room. I have loved you since the day I met you, when we were just children. Sometimes things that start rocky end up with the most wonderful conclusions. Sometimes we can't identify what makes us happy until we don't have it anymore. Piper, I know now what makes me happy, and I want to spend the rest of my life with you, cherishing you and loving you." Cody slipped the ring on her finger and held her hand as she spoke.

"Cody Micha Hughes. You are and will forever be my hero. I wouldn't be who I am today with our time together, despite the years in between. You have saved me, more than once, throughout my chaotic life, and have shown me the beauty of letting go. You, Cody, are my everything. I could never put into words how much your love has changed my life, though I hope to spend the rest of my days showing you."

Piper's tears finally overflowed, but she didn't stop to dry her eyes, instead she slid the ring onto Cody's finger and squeezed his hands tight. The officiant continued her script, and though it seemed to take forever, eventually pronounced them husband and wife. She nodded at Cody to kiss his bride, and instead of diving in, he wiped the tears from her cheeks with his thumbs, whispered something in her ear, and gave her a Hollywood movie kiss, which had the guests whooping and clapping in approval.

When Cody finally came up for air, he turned and smirked at Tanner standing off to the side of him, and grabbed Piper's hand and led her down the dock. "Wildflowers" by Tom Petty began over the speakers, at Melody's suggestion, and the two of them made their way up the terraces, stopping to give handshakes and hugs to the guests. Upon reaching the top, the newlyweds gave a brief wave and ran off down the path, holding hands and laughing.

Tanner moved to meet Melody in the middle of the dock, linking his arm with hers, and led her up the stairs. Having finished their ceremonial duties, they waited at the top for Jack and Riley, who had been sitting together in the front row. Jack winked at Melody as he approached, and she leaned into Riley's arms. Now she just had to give a perfect speech, one of her least favourite things in the world, with next to no prep time. Piper had been trying to do her a favour, but Melody thought her way of handling it was just the opposite.

They had a small window of time now to take photos, but the bride and groom were nowhere to be found. Melody guessed the couple had gone to another location for pictures and would return when the photographer needed her and Tanner to join them. There were drinks and camp-themed appetizers in-between, but Melody retreated to her cabin to freshen up instead.

Impressed with herself for not ruining her fancy makeup with tears, Melody found her hair still intact too, which relieved her. She put on an extra layer of deodorant for her nervous sweat and slid her Birks on to make a pit-stop in the bathroom. No matter how wild and free she felt while at camp, walking in a bathroom barefoot was beyond her comfort zone.

Melody dropped her Birks back off at the cabin and walked to the centre of camp with her rinsed and dried feet, now free of sand for the time being. Piper and Cody returned.

"It's time for photos," Piper called and waved the four of them over.

"Uh, I'm okay, I'll hang out here," Riley said, his voice steady but his body language screaming "nope"!

The photographer snapped away for the next half hour, getting various configurations of the friends and some family in each shot. When they finished, Melody gave Piper and Cody a big hug and told them their wedding location took the cake, how perfect their vows were, and how happy she was for them. The guys all made similar sentiments, and the group strolled back to the dining hall.

Melody played maid of honour again and checked on the food,

and when she came out and gave Piper a thumb's up, Piper dashed over to the camp bell and rang it long and loud to signal the meal. Everyone was already standing in front of her, but it was a fun detail to add to their wedding day.

Cody took it one step further, however, when he announced the guests should line up in front of their cabin names along the roofline, and they were going to sing grace on the porch. Melody giggled, and Tanner rolled his eyes. As if on cue, Jack ran up on the porch beside Cody to help lead grace. Deciding it was only fitting to sing Johnny Appleseed, they started with their arms in the air forming circles over their heads, and the anticipatory and drawn out "Oooh…" coming from behind their grins.

As even the non-camp attendees clapped their way through the grace, Melody's smile grew. All was right in the world, and she couldn't imagine being any happier than she felt at that moment.

CHAPTER 35
JUNE 2001
MELODY

The dining hall looked more beautiful than anything Melody had ever seen before. The sunset gave a stunning backdrop through the windows; glowing pinks and oranges over the lake. Along the middle of the wood tables were lace runners, topped with votive candles sprinkled between greenery native to the camp. There were two glasses per setting, one with water and one with champagne. Melody had never had champagne before, but she had recently adopted the famous, "I'll try anything once" mentality. Since the cabins already divided the guests into groups, assigned seating was unnecessary. Melody, Riley, Tanner, Jack, Piper, and Cody all shared a head table though, despite being split into three separate cabins.

Piper and Cody were the last to enter the dining hall. The speakers played The Beatles "In My Life" as they danced their way in holding hands. Piper pretended to try to beeline to her seat, but Cody lifted her hand, spun her around, and pulled her in for a slow dance while the song continued. They gazed at each other while shuffling their feet, and anyone paying any sort of attention knew that they both were enjoying the pure bliss of this moment.

As the music faded out, Cody and Piper finished their dance

with an impressive dip and everyone clapped. They beamed and bowed in jest before taking their seats. The kitchen staff began serving their unconventional wedding dinner. Turkey, mashed potatoes, stuffing, gravy, corn, and bread—all of Piper's favourites. Because of her upbringing, she had only experienced a handful of traditional holiday meals in her life, and her one request for the wedding was that they serve her favourite meal.

Jack remarked how the last time they all shared a meal together had been a similar harvest feast the previous year, and they sat with the irony for a moment.

"Well, dig in!" Piper exclaimed, too excited to wait any longer. The friends all chuckled as they picked up their forks.

"This has been the most perfect day," Melody said to the table.

"It has," agreed Tanner.

The dining hall was silent beyond the sound of forks and knives scraping against plates. As people finished their meals, Melody suggested she and Tanner should give their speeches, and Piper nodded, despite not putting her fork down for a second. Melody climbed out of the tight squeeze between the table and the bench, thankful again for her short dress, but cognizant of not raising her leg too high either, and moved to the front of the room. Tanner removed his jacket and followed close behind. They had agreed before the meal that they'd speak together, to make it a little less nerve-racking for them both.

"Hi everyone! For those that haven't met me, I am Melody, the maid of honour. Thank you so much for travelling great distances to celebrate this beautiful wedding! I have known Piper since we were preteens, sharing meals in this same building as campers at Camp Sweet Clover. Though, I have to say, I never imagined being back here over a decade later, giving a speech at her wedding! Piper's strength draws us all in, and I am so thrilled that she has found a worthy partner in Cody. It's incredible that they now get to enjoy their happily ever after. They both deserve every second of love they've found in each other! We should all be so lucky. To the bride and groom!"

She raised her glass of champagne and clinked her glass with Tanner before taking a sip.

"Well, I guess that leaves me. I'm Tanner, the best man. I have known Cody since he first came to Sweet Clover as a camper too. He was so shy when he arrived, but after I pulled him out of his shell, he became one of my best friends. From the day I met him, he has been head-over-heels for Piper, even before they were together, and despite the years between the beginning of their story and now, he never stopped loving her. I am confident that he will be by her side forever, and I can't wait to see where their lives will take them. Please join me in wishing the happy couple many years of love!"

The room raised their glasses again in celebration. Melody and Tanner retreated to the table, glad their official duties were done. Piper got up, quickly wiping a tear from her cheek, and Cody, holding his emotions back, stood and gave Tanner a firm hug. Piper wrapped her arms around Melody.

"The speech was perfect, thank you," she whispered in Melody's ear before grabbing Cody's hand and pulling him to the front of the room.

"We would like to say thank you for coming to celebrate our big day with us," Cody started, "and we appreciate those of you who had to travel long distances to be here."

"We have an announcement we would like to make too, while we have you all in one place," Piper said with a half-smile.

Melody's mind immediately jumped to them being pregnant, while the guys seemed clueless waiting for the news. *That would explain them moving up the wedding... how did I not think of it before?*

"Piper and I have talked a lot about how we want to start our lives, and what we want to do with our time," Cody began.

"And it wasn't difficult to decide when the perfect opportunity presented itself to us..." Piper trailed off, increasing the tension.

Cody finished her thought, "We are going to be taking over Camp Sweet Clover as the new directors!"

Several people gasped audibly, though no one looked more shocked than Melody. Her mouth had drawn up in a huge smile, though her eyes were still wide with surprise. Her second home that she loved so dearly was now in the family, and it filled her with joy. Everyone clapped.

"The camp will remain in the hands of the organization that has always owned it, but with their approval and help from the board of directors at The Rose Project, we have secured a government grant to make some changes. It will provide us with the funding we need to offer camp scholarships for preteens and teenagers with mental illnesses to attend the new retreat-style sessions we will offer one week a month every summer," Cody explained.

"We want Sweet Clover to be a safe haven for kids like me, who need a little more support than a traditional summer camp can offer. The camp experience can change lives, as I believe we have shown by example. You are here celebrating the by-product of Sweet Clover," Piper said as she squeezed Cody's hand.

Cody gestured to the head table and said, "Our best friends, Jack and Tanner, also exemplify beautiful relationships sparked at camp. And together with all our friends, we have kept this place alive in our hearts, even when we couldn't be here physically."

The room clapped again, and Piper waited for the applause to calm. "One more thing," she started, "none of us would be here without my friend Melody. She has done more for us than I can put into words, and she has dedicated her life to help those with mental illness. She has been studying to be a psychologist, and we hope that one day she will join us here at Sweet Clover as our on-site therapist."

All eyes were on Melody, as she attempted to hold her composure. Of all the things she expected to come out of this weekend, this was never even a consideration. With her jaw on the table, and in complete shock, she nodded at Piper. The room clapped again, and this time, Piper let them continue.

"Thank you so much for celebrating this day with us and thank you in advance for your support as we grow Camp Sweet Clover into something new and beautiful, while honouring old traditions too," Cody said, and they both stepped into Melody's arms, hugging them tight.

"I can't even string the words together to express how excited I am for this," Melody said to them both.

"Us too," they replied in unison.

The three walked back to the head table to high fives and hugs from their friends, but Riley just stared at Melody.

"Isn't this the best? I have a career that is better than anything I ever dreamed of, and I didn't even have to interview!" she laughed.

A career at Sweet Clover. It is almost too good to be true. Riley squeaked out a quiet congratulation through a forced smile.

"So, when do we start?" Melody asked, and the entire table laughed.

"Our takeover date is January 1st," Cody said.

"And for the first year or two, we will continue to run it as is. We want to get our feet wet, see what will work when bringing in our retreat weeks, and what doesn't and needs an alternative plan," Piper continued.

"That's perfect, because I still have to do my master's degree before I can get licensed. I've never worked with kids though, like you both have," Melody said, her face crumpled with worry.

"You can come hang out and work during the summer in another position, to get some camp experience under your belt," Cody suggested.

Melody's face lit up. Still trying to take it all in, she could barely contain her joy. The staff had cleared the tables, and many of the guests were heading back to their cabins to freshen up.

Melody looked at Piper with a smirk and said, "I am so excited. Do you know what I want to do right now?"

Piper stared back at her as if trying to read her mind. Somehow, their friendship had become strong enough that this was an actual possibility, and Piper took off running. Melody grabbed both bouquets from the table and chased after her. All the guys followed behind, though they kept to a moderate walking pace, wondering where the crazy women were going.

When they reached the terraces, Melody handed Piper her flowers like a baton and they slowed their pace to jog down the steps before grabbing each other's hands and running across the dock together. They had no concern for the steepness or the possibility of falling this time around. The guys looked on in shock from the top of the stairs, as both girls leapt, in their dresses, into the lake. The flowers floated in the ripples as the two of them surfaced among them.

That leap, unfortunately, would be the last picture-perfect moment the friends would see that weekend. Riley was cold and standoffish, growing more irritated by the minute. He hadn't even come to the reception for dancing and drinks; faking a headache and retreating to the cabin to go to sleep. Melody hadn't let it detract from her good mood, though.

In the morning, Riley's unhappiness with her summer job offer at Camp Sweet Clover was palpable. Melody was sure that was when his mood had changed, right after the announcement. She understood why; it would mean they would have to live at camp during the summer, or she would be there without him.

After watching her friends, who were so in love, get married, however, she could finally see the forest for the trees, and knew she had to let Riley go. She just didn't feel that way about him, and she had already been stringing him along for far too long.

"Riley, I understand you're upset about my job. I'm sorry. It was a complete surprise to me too. I had no idea they were doing this," Melody said as she got dressed.

"I just would have liked to have a conversation about it, instead of you accepting without even talking to me," Riley said.

"You're right, but they put me on the spot in front of an entire room full of people; what else could I do?"

"It's not just about the job, Melody. It's like I'm a background character in your life. I don't think that really works for me anymore."

"I know. I'm sorry. Maybe we let this go on far longer than it should have. You're incredible, Riley, but I think I need to be on my own right now. My life has gone in a completely different direction than I originally planned, and I want to, or need to, explore that."

Riley nodded and packed the last couple of things into his suitcase.

"I am happy for you and I want you to have everything you deserve out of life. I just wish that I could be a part of it," he mumbled to the floor.

"Thank you. I'm sure you'll find what you're looking for too," Melody said; carefully choosing her words to avoid any unintended implications, like she always did in their conversations.

Riley picked up his bag without another word and walked out of the cabin.

Flopping back onto her mattress, Melody expected to sink into feelings of guilt and sorrow, so why was she just wading? She guessed it confirmed everything she had already been thinking. *I should have let him go a long time ago. What was I waiting for?* Melody finished packing her suitcase, dreading the long drive home together. She left the cabin in search of TJ to see if they would mind giving her a lift instead, despite it being well out of their way.

Melody heard them before she saw them. Tanner and Jack were arguing, something she'd never seen before, in the overgrown pathway behind the dining hall, where no one ever ventured.

"You have got to be kidding me, Jack!" Tanner began. "We just settled down in Orillia. You love your job there; I love my job there. Now you're going to leave all that behind to come relive your glory days at camp?"

Melody stood frozen, knowing if she moved now, they might see her. She wanted to exit the area to give them privacy; not feeling even a hint of nosiness for once in her life, but the fear of being caught stopped her. Instead, she slowly crouched down like she was tying her shoe. *Not suspicious at all.*

"Tanner, I love this camp. I have always loved this camp. Coming back here is everything I could ever want," Jack explained.

"And what are you going to do for the other nine months of the year? We can't afford our new mortgage if you're only going to work for three months."

Melody didn't recognize this version of Tanner. He was always so free-spirited and so fun. There had probably been things going on behind the scenes that Jack, like always, had compartmentalized away from her.

"I haven't planned that far ahead, T. I'm as surprised as you that Piper asked me to come work too," Jack mumbled.

"That's not a good enough answer. This is our life you're uprooting, not only yours," Tanner said.

"I'm sorry, I'm sure you could come with me," Jack replied, but it wasn't enough.

"I have a career, Jack. Not all of us can follow anything that tickles our fancy at a moment's notice. I don't know how we can get through this with your blatant lack of regard for the life we're building together. I need some time," Tanner said, and walked off towards the water.

Melody watched in horror as Jack leaned back against the nearest tree and slumped to the ground, defeated. She wanted to run to him, to hug him, to comfort him, but she couldn't bear him knowing she'd seen the whole thing. Instead, she crept away to the front of the dining hall and sat on the porch. *Me and Riley aren't making it through this transition, but will Tanner come around and forgive Jack? How did this weekend end up so fractured when it started so perfectly?*

Maybe it all had been too good to be true after all.

June 22, 2002

Jack,

Today I packed up an entire season's worth of clothing, toiletries, and other various things into way too many suitcases. I had to play Tetris to fit them in my car! As I was organizing, I thought about the last time I packed for camp, for Cody and Piper's wedding. I had hoped for some understanding of my hesitation to commit after seeing Riley in my world. You were still with Tanner, two peas in a pod.

How did everything change so fast? How did our group become so broken, and how did this entire experience go from something so magical to being something fraught with hurt feelings, broken relationships, and no way through it all in one piece?

I know we have spoken very little recently. It felt important to give you your space as you navigated this major shift in your life. You must have been doing the same with me. I still can't believe you and Tanner couldn't work it out, even though you agreed to stay in Orillia for him. It honestly breaks my heart.

I guess now seemed like the best time to reach out, seeing as I'm leaving home for three months. I want to go back to Camp Sweet Clover with some semblance of peace, so I can see it as a fresh start there. I sure have tried to make a lot of those. Is there ever just too much history to reclaim the magic of a place?

It would be really cool if you came to visit this summer. I know after the whole Tanner thing you decided not to come, but you should reconsider, otherwise what did you lose Tanner for? There is plenty of extra room. I'm sure Piper and Cody would still let you work if you wanted to. We still don't have a decent instructor for that climbing wall, and we're always looking for more help. Think about it, okay?

I hope this letter finds you well, doing whatever makes you happy. You deserve a life filled with joy, despite what your brain might be telling you right now, and I want you to know that. I'll save a bunk for you at CSC if you ever want a change of scenery. I'd love to see you.

Melody

Melody arrived at Camp Sweet Clover after lunch on June 22nd. Driving in on the dirt road felt exactly how she remembered it, and despite some discomfort resurfacing from the last time she had been there, she vibrated with the excitement of returning. She decided that if she could work through the trauma of handling Piper's almost lifeless body; it would be a piece of cake to get over the most recent relationship-drama. She rolled her car window all the way down and breathed in. The early season's air had a damp, earthy scent; a detail she'd overlooked during the wedding, and she made a mental note to remember the distinctions of the changing seasons.

Melody kept mentally running through the upcoming schedule to make sure she wasn't missing anything. Her new position was as the volunteer coordinator until she could be the full time psychologist. Everything had come full circle. Alongside Piper, she would learn all the ins and outs of the staff side of camp life.

The rest of the employees would be arriving that day too, in time for their huge staff meeting, and they would take part in breakout training sessions over the following few days. Piper and Cody had been back and forth to camp since they took over in January, but the staff would need to spend a few days prepping the camp. That included cleaning all the buildings and checking every piece of equipment for anything that had fallen into disrepair over the winter. Their second week would end with a day of CPR and first aid training, a day of mental health first aid, facilitated by Melody because of her education, and a final staff meeting before the first campers arrived on July 6th.

It would be a hectic couple of weeks, but it would be so rewarding at the same time. Melody couldn't wait to meet all the staff and get familiar with them, especially their reasons for wanting to work at CSC. She imagined that many of them would share stories about how their camp experiences shaped their lives. It was only natural to choose work that ignited your passions. That's why she'd ended up there, after all.

Melody drove her car past the parking lot and all the way into camp. One of the best perks of being there for an extended period had to be the ability to drive as close to her quarters as possible to unload her three months' worth of belongings. Cody and Piper had given her a few options of where to make her home during that time, knowing the Fraser Bunkie bedroom wouldn't be big enough for her for an entire summer, and she decided that with her fresh start, she wanted to live somewhere she hadn't before. She chose the Poppies cabin, which sat atop the arts and crafts building, and had a beautiful balcony off the back overlooking the lake. When she came back in an official capacity, she planned to do a lot of art therapy with the campers—something she was going to be studying in her upcoming practicum—so she figured this was the perfect location for her forever-cabin. Not to mention the serenity of the view, and being off in the back corner of the camp, with only Marigolds and the cooks' cabin past hers.

The only downside to Poppies was the very steep set of stairs she had to navigate, so unpacking the car would be an enormous chore. Thankfully, Cody had seen her pull in and brought his muscles to help her.

"Melody!" he called as he ran towards her, scooping her up in a hug, and spinning her around.

Melody had spent a lot of time on the phone with Piper and Cody over the last year to plan how the camp was going to be run, and she and Cody had really grown their friendship over that time.

"Hey, friend! Are you going to help me with all these bags? I forgot how impossible these stairs were!" she said with a joking groan as he put her back on her feet.

"Cody Hughes at your service!" he exclaimed as he popped the trunk.

The two unloaded her car and carried what seemed like her entire life up the stairs, one bag at a time. Thankfully, it didn't take long between the two of them, though she still felt her heart racing as they hauled the last bag up, and she collapsed onto the bed. She looked at Cody, who sat down on the bed beside her. A smile played across his lips.

"What?"

"I'm just glad you're here, and Piper can't wait to see you!"

"Yes, where is Pipes?" Melody asked.

"She is up in the parking lot directing staff. She radioed me to say she saw you drive by."

"Sweet. I'll head up there after I've settled in. I don't want to leave all my unpacking until I come back at bedtime. I will be really mad at myself if I do that!"

"Cool, I'll catch you in a bit," Cody said as he took the stairs down two at a time, still having much more energy than she did.

Melody sat up and looked around the cabin. It was funny that she'd never stayed there in all her CSC adventures, but she looked forward to it this time around. Unpacking her bags and figuring out where everything should live required a little creativity, but once she had her clothes unloaded onto a few of the bunks and her stereo situated, she considered it enough progress, and stepped out onto the balcony.

She had a perfect sightline of the lake, and the view took her breath away. It was exactly what she had hoped for. She planned to spend mornings out there with her coffee, and then she'd enjoy the sunset over the lake while the campers were playing the wide game. She would get lots of journaling done during those times, decompress from long days in the sun, and plan the yet to be determined projects she would help volunteers with. The quiet, alone time would be vital to her enjoyment of the summer.

The cabin was the perfect choice. She took a deep breath in and exhaled all her hesitation about coming back, and descended the steps to find Piper. It occurred to her that running up and down the stairs for three months would get her into great shape. She giggled at the idea and wandered off to the parking lot.

Piper wasn't hard to spot amongst all the new staff milling around. She wore a sunflower yellow shirt that said Camp Sweet Clover on the front, and staff in huge letters on the back. As soon as she spotted Melody, she excused herself from her conversation, and sprinted towards her. They embraced with a long hug.

"Can you believe it?" Piper asked.

Melody looked around at all the young adults unloading their cars, and she really couldn't. She shook her head in response.

"Hey, I need to talk to you about something before I forget," Melody said.

"Sure, what's up?" Piper asked and led Melody over to the porch where it was quieter.

"I told Jack he should come visit in a letter I sent him this morning. I may have also mentioned there would be a place for him if he wanted to work. I hope that's okay. I think he's having a really tough time right now," Melody explained.

"Oh, sure," Piper said, feigning sarcasm.

"I should have spoken to you guys first..." Melody trailed off.

"It's fine," Piper said with a smile. "I invited him to come to work, anyway!"

Melody nodded and gave her another hug. "I'm so glad to be here," she gushed.

"It's going to be the best. Come help me direct these staff, okay?"

The women broke off and started showing the staff where to go.

Melody couldn't believe how young they all looked. She remembered being at Camp Sweet Clover as a camper and all the counsellors and other staff had seemed so grown up. Now it was the complete opposite. Had she gotten older or had the staff gotten younger? Either way, she didn't like it.

Melody would have lots in common with the staff, despite them seeming so young. She figured she'd be able to connect with them easily too. Camp people were camp people, after all.

She never felt as at ease with anyone as she did with CSCers. Were these young adults ready to handle all the rambunctious children headed their way, though?

Never mind the teens, were she and her friends ready? Although Melody lacked camp management experience, Piper's years of managing the shelter made her plenty qualified as the director. Cody also had experience managing a retail store and had worked with a lot of teens and young adults, so he was in his element. Outside of being Piper's co-director, he would spend most of his time as the activity coordinator, ensuring the campers were enjoying their time, with a variety of activities, including some of the friends' favourites from when they were campers.

Overall, between the three of them, they would figure this out. Of course, there was two weeks' worth of work to do first, so that was what she needed to focus on for now.

The time passed without too many snags, much to the surprise of the friends. They had scrubbed and organized all the buildings, which seemed daunting at first, but when divided up throughout the staff, it was quite an efficient project. The counsellors were to clean their cabins from top to bottom, and the kitchen staff oversaw the kitchen. All the specialized staff worked in their specific locations. The lifeguards took the waterfront shed, and the nurse took the nurse's station. Piper, Cody, and Melody took the dining hall, the Fraser Bunkie, the office, and the tuck shop. And everyone pitched in to do the bathrooms, staff building, and laundry room.

The training sessions also progressed without a hitch. Many of the staff came to camp already certified in CPR and first aid, but they sat in for a refresher course, anyway. Most of them had not had mental health first aid, though, which was nerve-racking for Melody. Kids trust their counsellors to help them during their camp stay, and she needed to implement this training efficiently to ensure the entire staff would rise to any challenge. Education like this would have been life-changing for Piper, and many others, in the summer of '94.

After training, they released the staff for some fun and relaxation before the first set of campers arrived. They could do any of the activities as long as they followed the rules and cleaned up after themselves, and it also allowed them to travel into town if they wanted to do any shopping.

On the night before the campers arrived, Piper, Cody, and Melody planned a huge staff party. They used the professional sound system installed for Piper and Cody's wedding the summer before, and they had the kitchen staff prepare a buffet style dinner with tons of foods they wouldn't be having during sessions because they were too expensive to prepare for the entire camp. Everyone ate, danced, got to know each other, and had an absolute blast.

The next morning, the three of them cleaned up the remnants from the party and sat down for their last management meeting before the campers arrived the following day. As they were discussing logistics of their first session, there came a knock on the office door. Melody, sitting closest to it, rose and pulled open the door, and got bowled over by the strongest bearhug she had ever received. She deduced without the help of her sight, who was doing the hugging, and a gentle joy overcame her; a feeling of bliss she couldn't quite explain.

When the arms released Melody from the hug, she was face to face with a bright, grinning Jack, and in that moment, everything was right in her world.

"Welcome to the team," Cody said.

"Are you staying? The entire season?" Melody asked.

"I hope you're prepared for a crash course today, campers arrive tomorrow," Piper informed him.

"I'm here as long as you'll have me," Jack replied to all three of their statements at once.

Melody threw her arms around him again and relief washed over her like the sun on your bare skin at the first hint of spring. She had been so excited to be back at Camp Sweet Clover, and so thrilled to be affecting the lives of so many young people, but being there without Jack just felt wrong. Like some tiny little voice in the back of her head was always telling her something was missing. Now with him here, that voice had disappeared.

"I missed you," she breathed with her arms still wrapped around him.

"Me too," he replied, not wanting to be too cavalier with his words.

"Well, we can continue this meeting later, Melody. Why don't you go give Jack a rundown of everything, and then he'll need you to train him for the mental health first aid. You will have a busy day ahead of you," Piper suggested.

"Campers arrive in T-26 hours!" Cody called after them as they left the office hand in hand.

As Melody and Jack walked up to the parking lot to grab his car, it occurred to her that Jack needed somewhere to live. The cabins were all in use, which meant either a bedroom in the Fraser Bunkie, which still held ominous vibes, or staying with her. She had plenty of room with an entire cabin to herself, however, she wasn't sure whether he would rather be alone, since it was for three months.

"So," Jack began, as if he could read her mind, "I'll need a bed. I don't want to be back in the bunkie, though. Those dang guitar lessons always wake me up on my day off," he said, eyes sparkling.

"Right?" Melody said with mock exaggeration. "Not a single

sleep-in to be had! Unfortunately, those are the only rooms we have left, unless you want to bunk with me?"

"Well, that depends…" Jack trailed off.

Melody's heart skipped a beat, despite her best effort to chill the heck out. "On what?"

"Which cabin you're in, of course!" Jack said with a cheeky smile.

"Oh, of course," Melody said, composing herself. "Poppies was the only logical choice."

"Agreed. Poppies is my favourite cabin. I will absolutely join you."

"Okaaay…" Melody drawled, "but no funny business!"

A laugh exploded from the depths of Jack's body, and Melody was so thrilled to see him happy again. While some part of them loved each other deeply, another part understood that any hint of intimacy would ruin everything, and they would lose the most important relationship of their lives.

It wasn't something they had ever spoken about, though Melody could tell that they both felt it in their bones. Their kind of soulmates came with a fine line to walk between best friends and, well, more than that, though somehow, they both seemed to recognize that there wasn't an option to cross it.

It had taken Melody years to get to this place with her feelings for Jack, especially after their tandem relationship-ending arguments the day after Cody and Piper's wedding. Melody knew it was the right choice though, so she kept that part of her heart compartmentalized from the rest of her life—she had learned from the best.

She wasn't sure if she would ever find someone she would be with forever, and she couldn't predict if Jack would either, but she had to be okay with all the potential outcomes for them both. As long as they were in each other's lives, she would be okay.

Jack parked the car in front of the Poppies cabin, and hopped out, then hauled his bags up the stairs two at a time.

"Okay, show-off. You think there's a badge for that?" Melody joked.

He chuckled and moved even faster. Melody was relieved he hadn't been there while she struggled to get hers up, one by one. *How embarrassing.* Of course, Jack had packed much lighter than she had and only made two quick trips up the stairs. When he finished, they sat down on the two twin counsellor beds facing each other.

The silence between them seemed to stretch on for hours, though it wasn't uncomfortable.

"You're my favourite person," Jack said, completely sincere for once in his life.

"You're my person," Melody offered in return.

There was no favourite designation needed. He was her only person; he always had been.

"I love you," Jack said to the floor without lifting his eyes to hers.

Melody's breath hitched as she let the words escape her lips for the first time in her life, "I love you too."

ACKNOWLEDGMENTS

This story began long ago in a faraway place, before I could see the forest for the trees. Publishing your very first novel isn't always wise, but *There's a Badge for That* was meant to be my debut. This process might have taken me a considerable amount of time, and a couple of massive perspective shifts, but I am so thrilled to release this story into the world, finally.

I need to start off by acknowledging that this book was a group project. The number of hearts and hands that helped me bring it to this point is immeasurable. I want you to know—yes, you—that your presence in my history, no matter how brief, weaved itself into the fabric of my life story, and that story bleeds between the fictional threads on these pages.

There is, of course, a list of people I'd like to thank specifically. Please don't expect an expertly crafted Academy Award speech. I'm attempting vulnerability and, well, I don't have a publicist to finesse it.

To my best friend and partner, Jesse, without whom this truly wouldn't have been possible. I know everyone says that, but you gave 110% every day to ensure I had the time and space to create this *work of heart*. Writing over 60,000 words in 30 days, during a worldwide pandemic necessitating the homeschooling of our three children, while chronically ill, and grieving the devastating loss of my mum, was impossible, and yet, somehow, you helped make it happen. You have been my biggest cheerleader since day one, despite the speed at which I flit from one idea to the next, and your encouragement pushed me to continue each time I lost hope along the way. You're the real MVP.

To my kiddos; Oliver, Reid, and Sawyer. You are my greatest joy and my biggest inspiration. Cheesy, right? I want nothing more than to make you proud, and to show you that you can achieve your dreams, even with every conceivable obstacle in your way. I can't wait to watch you live out your passions, and celebrate each of your accomplishments.

To my family; Dad, Mum (I know you're celebrating with a glass of champers somewhere), Andrea, Kirsten, Ann, and Neil. Thank you for sending me to summer camp, critiquing query letters, fact checking my medical references, babysitting the kids, and supporting me even when it felt like this book would *never* come to fruition.

To my cover designer, Christian Storm, thank you for your endless patience and willingness to make my vague ideas into a beautiful reality. To all those who acted as mentors, editors, beta readers, critique partners, idea contributors, and supporters; Karen, Katie, Cara, Sam, Kaitlyn, Diane, and Bree. Thank you for helping me become a better writer, and encouraging my continued work towards making this novel the best it could be. I would not be writing this acknowledgments page without your help—maybe I should have asked for your help here too.

And Mikey. Over 20 years ago, you cheated in your own gift exchange to ensure I would end up with a beautifully inscribed first edition of *The Perks of Being a Wallflower*, and I truly believe it changed the trajectory of my life. I am forever grateful. I may have written *my* story all over these pages, but none of it would exist without you. Our friendship is a lifeline I carry in my back pocket, mostly lived out through tiny screens to span the distance, though I know you're never further away than some rivers and roads. Thank you for always knowing what I need to hear, but telling me the truth instead. There must be a badge for that.

xo Relly

ABOUT THE AUTHOR

Relly Moring is a young adult author of hard-hitting, queer, contemporary novels. They are the partner of a lumberjack math-whiz, and the parent of three feral children, but they've also been a postpartum doula, an axe-throwing coach, a photographer, a babywearing educator, a music journalist, a nightclub drink-slinger, and an artisan of magickal spell jars and other witchy wares your parents would condemn. They do their best writing in impossible circumstances, like amid a worldwide pandemic while homeschooling their children, battling chronic illnesses, and grieving loved ones, *all at once*. Relly has a penchant for platonic soulmates and writes characters with turbulent histories and sunshiny story arcs. There are a few hills they will die on, but you can pry the Oxford comma from their cold, dead hands.

RESOURCES

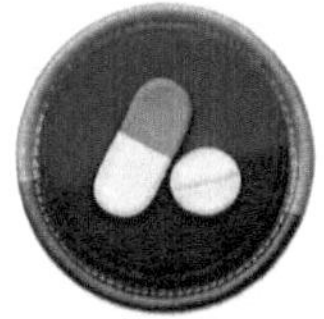

MENTAL HEALTH RESOURCES

- Suicide & Crisis Helpline North America: 9-8-8
- Kids Help Phone Canada: 1-800-668-6868
- Shout Helpline UK: Text "Shout" to 85258
- Canadian Mental Health: CMHA.ca/find-help
- Mental Health America: MHANational.org/get-help

SAFETY RESOURCES

- Sexual Violence Helpline Canada: 1-888-933-9007
- Domestic Violence Hotline USA: 1-800-799-7233
- Sexual Assault Helpline USA: 1-800-656-4673
- Domestic Abuse Hotline UK: 0808 2000247

2SLGBTQIA+ RESOURCES

- Trans Lifeline Canada: 1-877-330-6366
- Trans Lifeline USA: 1-877-565-8860
- The Switchboard UK: 0800 0119 100
- It Gets Better Canada: ItGetsBetterCanada.org
- It Gets Better USA: ItGetsBetter.org
- The Trevor Project USA: TheTrevorProject.org/get-help

LINKS

This is the end of *There's a Badge for That*, but it's not the end of the road for us. It would mean the world to me if you take two minutes to rate this book on Goodreads by scanning the QR code.

Any reviews, positive or negative, help readers like you find their next favourite book! You can also copy and paste it onto your purchase site to double your impact.

If you're interested in seeing future announcements before the public, or becoming a beta reader and receiving FREE advance copies of new releases, head to my website, RellyMoring.ca, and sign-up for my newsletter. No spam, I promise!

goodreads.com/RellyMoring
facebook.com/AuthorRellyMoring
instagram.com/RellyMoring
youtube.com/@RellyMoring